JUST TO SEE YOU

Second Edition

Cover art created with Leonardo Ai and Book
Brush

ISBN: 978-0-6458296-2-4

Connell Publishing

JUST TO SEE YOU

HELENA CARMICHAEL

PROLOGUE

Monday 19 September

Ally first noticed the two men out of the corner of her eye, as you'd notice a fully clothed person at the beach. She dismissed the start of alarm her heart gave as the result of too many months of suspicion and fear. She was jumping at shadows, every corner seemed threatening, every stranger dangerous. "Snap out of it," she told herself. "Nothing is going to happen now. It's over."

The fresh September breeze ruffled Ally's soft brown hair as she lifted her face to the warm sun and with a sigh, said a silent goodbye.

Ally was finally admitting defeat. She had tried so hard to continue her life in Australia, the country she and Luke had loved so much. But since her husband's murder it had become increasingly difficult. Maybe if she had been alone, it would have been worth the fear to stay, but she was unwilling to take the risk for someone else, someone small and vulnerable. So, she had gratefully accepted her parents' invitation to come home to Vancouver. They would be surprised when she arrived earlier than expected but pleased too. If there was one thing, she was certain of, it was their welcome. Despite the geographical distance, they had always been close.

Ally resisted the urge to glance at the two men. No one knew she was here. Bending down, she reached into the back seat and met the serious blue eyes of her baby, Nicholas. Focusing on his mother, he dissolved into a wide toothy smile that lit up his whole face. His Paw Patrol jumper and tiny jeans were still mercifully clean.

"Hello, my little man," Ally smiled back, the sadness and worry fleeing her expression at once, "let's get you out of that seat."

As soon as she unsnapped the buckle of his safety harness, Nicky started to wriggle and squirm until he was free. Ally grasped her baby's sturdy little body and hugged him to her. His arms wrapped around Ally's shoulders as he settled against her with accustomed contentment. A quiet happiness stole over her. Ally lifted him out of the car, navy dress swirling almost to her ankles as she looked around her.

The two men were closer now, casually looking at cars in the long-term parking lot. One was tall and thin, with a brown, pinched face and the other was small, soft and bald. They both wore identical black suits which made them look equally ridiculous and vaguely sinister. They drew nearer, seemingly loitering.

Ally felt a prickle of awareness run down her spine. Something was wrong. Hurrying now, she slung her inflight cabin bag onto her right shoulder while Nicky perched on her left hip. Gripping the handle of her large suitcase tightly, she started rolling it across the bitumen. If they could just get into the airport building, they would be safe. Leafy plane trees trembled gently above, and the car park loomed vast and deserted.

She didn't even hear their footsteps until they were upon her. Off balance, she tried to turn but the tall man had grabbed her hair and started yanking it backwards. Tears sprang into her eyes with the pain. Pudgy soft hands pushed between Ally and Nicky and started dragging him away from her. Ally dropped the suitcase and wrapped both arms around him so tightly that he protested.

Ally screamed, willing someone to come and help her and instead received a stinging backhander across her cheek from the short man. With dimming vision, she held on with all her strength. Beads of sweat glistened on the pasty face, studded with small shiny eyes which stared impassively at her, over Nicholas' head. Nicky was crying now, little choked off cries of fear.

Ally bent her head down as far as she could, trying to shield him from the attack. They would not even let her do that. A sharp tug on her hair brought her level with a semi-automatic that was even now swinging towards her temple. Held painfully by the tall man, she could only wait helplessly for the blow. Pain exploded in her brain then the sky turned grey and started to shrink. She felt herself slipping into unconsciousness.

Keep fighting, she told herself, don't give up, don't let them take Nicholas. But her body would not respond. She felt her grip on her precious child loosen and he was snatched from her just before she hit the pavement.

Chapter One

Brisbane

A sea of eyes was staring down at her and she couldn't breathe. Lying sprawled out in front of dozens of strangers, one shoe off, dress twisted and pulled up. It was like being caught in a particularly embarrassing nightmare, except for the throbbing pain in her temple which told her this was no dream.

Then she remembered. The airport. Nicholas. Through the waves of dizziness and pain, Ally fought to get up. It had been an empty car park, but her screams had brought help. Too late.

"My baby!" she gasped. "Someone took him."

A murmur passed through the crowd of onlookers. Ally searched their eyes. They held expressions of curiosity, concern and maybe pity. Then her gaze stilled on a pair of stormy grey eyes that held something else, knowledge, frustration and anger. They belonged to a striking man who was breathing hard as if he had been running. There was a sense of purpose about him that set him apart from the curiosity seekers. Just as she started to get up someone slipped in front of him and he disappeared.

Hands helped to lift her as the crowd began to react. Someone even put her shoe back on. Everyone was talking at once as word of the abduction spread.

"Call the ambulance," a middle-aged executive called as he bent to look at Ally's battered face.

"The police," another bystander yelled.

"And please hurry." Ally rasped. Fear had made her throat suddenly dry.

She stood shakily and pushed through the onlookers to her car. Nicky's baby seat sat empty in the back and her luggage lay on the ground where she had dropped it. Any hope Ally had that it had just been her imagination faded. After throwing the bags into her boot, she stopped. Lost, she just stood there. A gentle hand touched her shoulder and she turned to see a beautifully groomed flight attendant behind her.

"Do you need any help?" the woman asked with visible concern.

"Yes, yes I do," Ally replied. "Someone has taken my baby boy. Two men in dark suits. Did you see them?"

"No, I'm sorry, I didn't." The flight attendant turned to the others and asked them the same question. No one had seen anything. "Let's get you inside, maybe the security people can help."

The crowd had already started to thin as Ally was led into the airport lounge by the attendant. She barely noticed the ride along the escalator or the two-storey high crystal mural that greeted visitors. She walked numbly past the ticket offices and the rows of seats, beside tourist shops and down the steps to the customs area. Her mind kept replaying the moment when Nicholas was taken from her arms. Arms that ached with loneliness. Someone had already alerted airport security and a blue uniformed guard met them and took Ally to a mercifully quiet room to the right of the teeming departure gates.

The small room was thick with the smell of new carpet and fresh paint. Ally took in a deep breath of fumes, then sneezed. Her head was starting to hurt again, just above her left eye. She felt gingerly along her scalp. No hair missing. She rubbed her forehead, trying to think through the pain.

Nicky was gone. She should be out there searching the carpark, not sitting in a stuffy little room, isolated, useless. The security guard left for a moment and returned with a paper cup of cool water. Looking into his kind crinkled face Ally sipped. The water felt wonderful on her parched throat.

"Try not to worry too much, Ma'am. I've already called the feds. They have an office downstairs, there are a couple of them on duty 24/7 here," he told her. "Now just relax, take your time, and tell me what happened."

Curiously, his gruff voice did start to relax her. She let out a shuddering breath. Just as she started to explain, the door opened, and two police officers entered. The senior partner was a capable looking woman with a short, asymmetric cut who introduced herself as Sergeant Donna Marshal and Ally found herself liking the other woman immediately. She inspired confidence. Her partner's name was John Harrison, a tall, well-built and impossibly young constable. An army style short back and sides made him look like a raw recruit. "Ma'am," he nodded seriously as he sat down. Ally nodded back, saying nothing. Constable Harrison pulled out a tablet and prepared to take notes.

"Since your son was abducted at an international airport, it is our jurisdiction as Federal Police," Donna explained.

"Oh my God! Do you think they have taken him out of the country?" Ally shivered, despite the heat in the tiny room.

"Frankly, I doubt it. We put out a priority one alert as soon as we were notified of your son's abduction. There were only two flights we missed. Qantas to London and Cathay to Hong Kong but we have contacted the captains of each and there are no children on board. Passengers will be re-checked by the flight crew in the air. Airport security and the local police are screening all outgoing travellers as we speak. You are extremely lucky in a way Mrs Reed because we were already on the scene in the departure lounge doing security checks in liaison with customs."

"Yes, lucky..." Ally echoed. How could anyone call her lucky, she wondered. In her life luck had been fleeting.

"Sorry," Ally murmured as she realised Sergeant Marshal was talking to her. "Could you give me a description of your baby, Mrs Reed?" Understanding clouded the policewoman's open features as she repeated herself, more gently this time.

Ally nodded. "He is eighteen months old. He has light brown hair and blue eyes." Just like his father, she added mentally with a stab of pain.

"And your husband is...?" Donna didn't finish the question, but her tone implied, did Ally think that her husband was involved? She had read of cases where divorces had turned ugly and one parent had abducted the children.

"He's dead," she replied tonelessly, her green eyes lifeless. She was no longer looking at the policewoman, instead she saw something white lifting in front of her eyes. Luke's face lay there, crusted blood around his beautiful nose and mouth, beneath the sheet at the morgue. "He's dead," she whispered as Sergeant Marshal came back into focus.

"I'm sorry," the policewoman apologised. "Is there anyone we could contact for you now?"

Ally tried to concentrate on what the policewoman was asking her, but the pain refused to go. Sometimes she felt an overwhelming anger, rage even, that he had left her alone with a three-month old baby. No one to help with the midnight feeds. No one to talk to. No one to hand Nicky to and say "Here, he's been crying all day and I don't know what he wants or what to do!" No one to lean on, no one to tell you that you've done a great job.

Then the guilt would come as certainly as rain drops fall onto the hot earth. Guilt for the anger and self-pity. Guilt for the one being allowed to live while he had to die a frightening and lonely death. But the one constant feeling Ally lived with was pain. Only when she was concentrating on Nicholas could she hold it at bay, but at night, when she was alone in her bed, it would engulf her. How she missed him. He was not only her husband, he was her best friend, her confidante.

"No not really, my parents live in Canada and my business partner is in Europe on a buying trip. We own an interior design business and she does all the travelling. I wouldn't want to worry her, there's nothing she could do anyway. We've shut up shop for a few weeks, so there really is nobody."

Although Ally and Louise were friends and partners for a long time now, they couldn't have been more different. Ally was quiet and introverted. She had preferred to stay home even before she had met Luke, but Louise had a vast network of friends who helped her party away the free hours of the week. *AMH*

None of those friends really interacted with Ally, and she didn't really want them to, but today they would have come in handy. If this had happened to Louise, she would have had all the support she needed. Ally was going to have to cope alone.

Constable Harrison wrote careful notes on his tablet. Clumsily Ally rifled through her overflowing shoulder bag, finally pulling out her phone. It was full of pictures of Nicholas: with Ally holding him, sleeping on his father's chest, smiling up at her from his cot. She scrolled through until she found the latest. Just this morning in his Paw Patrol sweater.

Tears welled in her eyes and her fingers shook as she handed Donna her phone.

Luke's death was so shattering that Ally had wanted to die with him. Nicholas had been her only reason to pick up the pieces of her life. It had taken over half a year, but slowly she had started to live rather than exist from minute to painful minute. Then the terror had started again. Ally had thought running to the other side of the world, into the safety of her parents' arms could save them. She had been wrong.

"What had the two men looked like?" Donna questioned and Ally described them as best as she could. Their faces were etched in her memory.

"Do you know of any reason why someone would take your son?"

"No, not really..." Ally wasn't ready to voice the suspicion that the man behind this could be part of her own family and would not hesitate to kill Nicholas if it suited him any more than he would hesitate to crush a fly. *♔♕♘*

The questions continued interminably and the air in the little room became stifling. Finally, it was over. Ally was asked not to talk to the reporters outside until a press conference could be arranged the next morning. That would give maximum media coverage to the abduction and alert the whole country. She felt wrung out and reaction was starting to set in. Part of her wanted to sit in the straight-backed vinyl chair until this nightmare was over, the anxiety was giving her waves of goosebumps and nausea, but she knew she had to get up and go. She was totally alone now. There was no one on whom she could lean on, let alone trust. Max Reed had "friends" everywhere. The tentacles of his power had reached out and destroyed their little family. Even that was not enough for him. Now he was playing with the life on an innocent child. He probably thought that a mother would do anything to protect her baby. He was right. But why? She had done nothing to him. They had not even met. It was as if her mere existence was enough to enrage him.

Ally felt despair creeping in. She smoothed her dress over her hips as she stood up. Wearily she left the little room and started down the corridor towards the airport lounge, a small solitary figure. The cloak of loneliness she had known before meeting Luke had returned like an old friend. The sky through the glass walls had darkened to indigo. She and Nicholas should have been over the Pacific Ocean by now, with nothing more to worry about than airline food and boredom.

Melbourne

Today was the culmination of years of thought and months of planning. He loved the fear he could create simply by pulling a few strings. He saw himself as a puppeteer whose puppets did not even know who he was or why their lives were being destroyed.

He smiled. The banker's lamp shone steadily on the huge mahogany desk and glinted off his silver topped cane. Many rows of books lining the library walls were bathed in the soft glow of the open fire. Despite the warmth, the old man always felt cold here, his bones ached. With effort, he stood and walked to the large picture window. Leaning heavily on the cane, he watched the late afternoon sun playing silently over the leafy garden. Spring had covered the hundred-year-old oaks and maples with myriads of tiny bright green shoots. He enjoyed watching the garden from the warmth of the library, but never went outside when he was home. The air had a frosty bite that reminded him that there were some things that he could not control.

An industrious gardener scurried across his field of vision, head down, as if aware of the eyes observing him. The old man smiled grimly. That was the way good employees should act.

14

A discrete knock sounded through the heavy door and his secretary entered. He was a small, thin man who seemed to fade into any background. A useful creature who was inclined to be slightly afraid of his boss. The old man turned from the window, so his face was shadowed while his white hair glowed in a sinister halo. The secretary nervously cleared his throat before beginning his report. All had gone well, according to plan. The baby was being taken north. The police knew nothing.

"Good, I want my plane ready immediately, this requires my immediate attention."

"Yes sir!" the secretary replied, leaving the room as quickly as he dared. As he pulled the door closed, he gave a small sigh of relief. Evil was a tangible thing in that room. You could almost smell it, along with the inevitable stuffy odour of rubbing alcohol, camphor and death. One day he would conquer his fear and leave, but not today.

A few patient reporters and photographers milled about in the airport lounge and Ally was able to observe them for a few moments before they spotted her. It gave her time to square her shoulders, mentally preparing herself for more questions. She wasn't prepared, however for the dark figure that detached itself from the shadows of the corridor to fall into step beside her.

Starting violently, she turned to look up into the grey eyes belonging to the man she had noticed in the car park that afternoon. For a split second, she felt as if she was falling again, before the world righted itself. The intensity in his eyes had been dimmed by fatigue and his well-cut suit was decidedly crumpled. If Ally had been at all interested in men, which she wasn't, then she would have found him incredibly attractive.

He moved with a deceptively casual ease as he walked with her into the glare of the waiting area. One of the reporters looked around and saw her. As one, galvanised into action they quickly surged towards her, firing questions as only stunningly slim blondes with extreme self-confidence can. Suddenly Ally felt her elbow taken in a firm comforting grasp by the man beside her. He raised his hand. The simple gesture quietened the reporters immediately. The stranger looked as if he was accustomed to being obeyed without question.

"It's been a long day guys, how about giving the lady a break?" he suggested quietly, and everyone stilled.

Ally started feeling annoyed, a welcome shot of something other than anxiety. Why was he speaking for her when she didn't even know him? But she was so tired, that he was speaking again before she could even form a retort.

"Thank you for your patience, everyone, there will be a press conference tomorrow morning. I hope to see you all there."

She tried to free her elbow from its warm prison, but short of causing a scene, there was nothing she could do. The man at her side guided her through the throng and out into the twilight. The sound of a plane taking off rent the air. Once outside he lengthened his pace, half dragging Ally in his wake.

"Where do you think you're taking me?" she demanded, wrenching her arm away. His grip loosened immediately and she almost fell. Rubbing her elbow, even though he hadn't hurt her, she felt the memory of his touch on her skin. Ally glared at his outline in the gloaming.

"We've got to get you home before you collapse," he replied tolerantly. She noticed his voice again. It was the sort of voice you could listen to all day, deep and slow and a little rumbly. She felt like closing her eyes and letting him talk to her so she could forget the terror for just a while. She shook the feeling off silently berating herself – this man could be connected to the kidnappers. She would disappear and no one would even know.

"I'm not going home with you!" Ally felt her voice rising.

"Would you rather go and get something to eat?" he asked with a trace of concern.

"No!" Ally almost shouted.

"Well home it is."

"You've got to be kidding." Ally struggled to keep her temper. After all that had happened today, she felt herself teetering on the verge of hysteria. This reasonable sounding, calm stranger seemed to be expecting her to follow him blindly. His complete confidence only made her angrier.

"Look, I don't know who the hell you are, and I'm not going home or anywhere else with you, so leave me alone!"

The amusement fled from his face.

"I'm sorry. I saw what happened in the carpark and I think I can help you get your little boy back, but we have to talk." His voice dropped. "Alone."

That changed everything. Ally looked at him searchingly in the fading light. It was too dark to make out his expression. She saw a man in his mid-thirties, maybe, with slightly messy dark hair that looked as though he habitually combed it back with his fingers. Seconds later he confirmed this by tiredly running his hand through his hair. Somehow that movement made him seem more human. Instinctively and despite her better judgement, Ally felt she could trust him. She stood silent for a long moment, deciding, then with a sigh, she nodded.

Besides, there were a few questions that needed to be answered.

His car was a sleek silver fastback. Of course, it was. He opened the wide passenger door and Ally sank gratefully into the black leather seat. The cocoon of comfort soothed her jagged nerves and she felt exhaustion creeping in over the anxiety of losing Nicky.

"By the way, the name's Jim Conrad." He introduced himself as they pulled out of the parking lot and swung onto the exit lane.

"Alexandria Reed, you can call me Ally." She was too tired to say anything else. The warmth in the car was lulling her off to sleep. Darkness hid the industrial countryside through which the road curved gently before joining the massive Gateway Bridge.

Ally stared unseeingly into the darkness, seeing another night when she first held Nicky's warm, tiny body. The joy that had filled her whole being from the time she had found out she was pregnant, and continued for nine months, erupting into hot tears as he lay on her chest. The instinct to protect him had been so strong. She begged Luke to go with the nurses as they took the newborn baby to get weighed just in-case they lost him. She didn't leave his side in the months that followed.

Nicholas was such a beautiful baby that people stopped her in the supermarket to coo at him. It made her watch him even more closely. When Ally returned to work, she couldn't make herself trust a babysitter and had taken him into the store with her, squeezing a crib and then a playpen in amongst the bolts of fabric and wallpaper. She and Louise had hit on the idea of expanding into nursery decorating. It was a great success. All in all, Nicholas had adapted to her life remarkably well and Luke's also. He doted on his young son.

They were such a small but happy family, the three of them. Ally had known that Luke had family in Melbourne but he didn't talk about them much. The past had painful, tragic memories that Luke seemed anxious to keep in the past. He was content with the present. Her husband had been a master craftsman. He worked in a small exclusive furniture factory hand building magnificent sideboards with intricate detailing down to the last dovetail joint.

They had met at the annual antiques fair at the Brisbane City Hall. Ally had noticed the serious sandy haired man examining a writing desk with unusual intensity, looking at the details with a magnifying glass. Intrigued, she forgot about bidding for the chaise her client had specifically requested and watched him in rapt attention.

As one of the partners of a successful interior design business, Ally spent a lot of time at auctions. She noticed Luke there on two more occasions before summoning up the courage to introduce herself. Their common interest in furniture gave them an easy way to become acquainted. After that she used his furniture in some of her bigger projects. Their easy friendship grew into love and they spent every spare moment together.

Within two months, they had had a quiet ceremony and become husband and wife. Both loners, each felt completed by the other. Nicholas added to that completeness. Luke usually managed to come to her store for lunch, or they would meet in the park. He couldn't stand being separated from his wife and baby boy for even a day. Sometimes in the dead of night, Ally would wonder what had happened to Luke when he was younger and she would listen to his uneven breaths and incomprehensible groans as he slept. She knew that when daylight came, she would not have to heart to ask him. It was the only thorn in their marriage. He never confided in her, never let her into the dark corners of his mind.

Then one evening, after they had shared a bottle of red wine on their anniversary, he had let the truth out, almost unconsciously, and the horror of it had frightened her. The next day he acted as if nothing had happened and she took his lead even as her heart bled. That is how she guessed who was behind the abduction. Otherwise, she would have been completely ignorant.

But for the moment she had to wait. Someone else was holding all the cards and if she tried to confront the man that she suspected was responsible, there was no telling what he would do to Nicholas. She could only pray that her little boy was safe.

Ally looked at her watch. She had not made lunch or dinner for Nicky and it was way past his bedtime. The realisation crept over her like a cold wind. She could no longer bury herself in the past, hide in the memories. Those men would have no idea what to feed a baby, how to look after him. What would they do when he cried and cried for his mother in the middle of the night? Would they walk with him until he fell asleep or would they get frustrated? Ally's mind shied away from that thought. Max Reed would only hire professionals, men who could cope with any situation and not fall apart if a baby cried. She had to keep herself from falling apart too. She just couldn't help thinking that those men had not looked as if they enjoyed the company of small children and animals.

The city loomed ever closer. Traffic was still congested despite the evening hour. Horns sounded here and there as cars jostled for position. Jim Conrad showed no impatience. His calmness steadied her and she looked out of the window. They had almost reached the Story Bridge. Jewel bright multicoloured lights flickered and reflected off the dark still water of the river that coiled around the city like a sluggish snake. By day the river was mud brown and the city was plain and hazy in the heat but at night its magic showed and for Ally it was the most beautiful river in the world.

The interior of the car could not quite exclude the faint tinkling of music and laughter as people on a boat cruise glided past the restored Port Building. They seemed like inhabitants of another world, a carefree, happy one, quite unlike Ally's world. At any other time, she would have wanted to linger, to absorb the sights and sounds. Now she just wanted to get home, away from them, for their happiness only intensified her panic and misery. Maybe it was all a sick joke, maybe Nicholas was at home waiting for her. Maybe she was having a nightmare. God knows she had had her fair share of them over the last few months. No, this was no nightmare. This was worse. There was no way to wake up from this one.

"Where do you live? the man by her side softly broke into her thoughts.

"Greyson Road, Hill End," she replied. Privately, she thought he knew very well what the address was. Brisbane is the sort of city that baffles outsiders. Built in the early days of convict settlement when town planning took second place to topography, it has long winding roads which change names at bends or corners so one road can have four or five names. If you take the wrong turn you can end up lost and miles out of the way. Added onto at random, suburbs radiate in all directions from the winding river and up and down the hills and valleys. It is a sprawling city of over two and a half million people with a massive surface area.

Once Ally had taken the wrong road, or rather the right road in the wrong suburb and had ended up staring at Moreton Bay, when she was supposed to be at a party clear across town in Mount Nebo to the north. Laughing at herself, she bought fish and chips and sat on the Shorncliffe pier and ate them, the party forgotten. The memory brought a ghost of a smile.

Jim definitely knew where he was going. He had skilfully threaded his way through the evening traffic out of the Valley and onto the massive iron Story Bridge. Ally always felt nervous on the bridge trying to choose the correct lane because it was almost impossible to change by the time the signs became visible. She wasn't a bad driver but some situations made her uneasy. Unlike the man at her side, she guessed. Every inch of him exuded quiet confidence. Jim had unhesitatingly taken the centre right lane, the lane that led specifically to the inner western suburbs. Where Hill End perched on the bank of the Brisbane River like a tiny peaceful haven. The GPS was off.

Ally suddenly realised how terribly vulnerable and stupid she was. She really did not know this man at all, this perfect stranger knew where she lived. He probably knew she lived alone with her baby. She twisted her wedding ring around and around but it brought her no comfort, only a dull empty ache where her heart should have been.

Thoughtfully Ally studied his profile. She saw that his brown hair had been lightened by fresh air and sunshine, but his eyebrows were straight and dark. He had a strong face, well proportioned, with a long straight nose and an impossibly chiselled jaw. His lips were firm and moulded, with no hint of amusement now.

If Jim knew he was being assessed, he gave no hint of it. His hands rested relaxed on the steering wheel.

"You'll have to take the next right at Vulture Street," Ally directed unnecessarily.

After that she lapsed into a pensive silence as Jim gave up the pretence of not knowing where she lived. They stopped for groceries at a small store in West End before driving further along shorter, narrower convoluted streets to the tiny suburb of Hill End, perched high above the Brisbane River. The house seemed reassuringly normal. Was it only this morning that Ally had left, full of hope? Determined to start afresh, to go home.

Jim pulled up in front of her small house.

"You may as well park off the street," Ally offered, "the young fellow two doors up from us had his car stolen a few weeks ago by joy riders. Eventually, they did return it, minus the seats and with a few extra dints."

"Sounds like a nice neighbourhood," Jim commented dryly.

"It's not usually that bad," Ally replied defensively. Then added, "you will need to turn sharply to miss the gate post."

"Thanks."

He manoeuvred the sleek car effortlessly down the steep driveway and under the highset house. Jim had never lived in a house. Apartments were more to his liking. They did not feel as empty when you lived alone. But this house was certainly beautiful. Small, but perfectly proportioned, even in the dark. The front of the house sat low to the ground with only enough clearance for the fastback, but at the back the underside of the house towered above them.

It was a typical Queenslander with wide, low-slung verandas on three sides letting cool air circulate. Flowering vines climbed delicately through the iron lacework scenting the night air with sweetness.

Jim silently followed Ally up the fifteen back steps and saw her fingers trembling as she turned the key in the lock. The door swung in on well-oiled hinges. He gently held her to one side and preceded her into the dark corridor, leaving the bag of groceries in the hall. Silently motioning for her to wait, Jim checked each room. Only when he was satisfied that nobody waited in the shadows, did he let her turn on the lights.

Ally said nothing. She merely watched his thorough, professional movements. How many times had she come home after dark with Nicholas, afraid of the shadows in her own home? She told herself she was being silly and irrational. Seeing this man search her home for intruders gave her own fears substance, justification even.

It was good to have someone else do the worrying for once. It would be easy to become reliant on a strong male figure like this Jim Conrad and she would have to guard against that. It had been too difficult the first time, after Luke died. She had been left with a household to run, a baby to look after singlehandedly, a business. She had to work hard, but it brought an unexpected reward. Independence. She found inner strengths she had not known were possible. Over the months she had fought fatigue, fear, the mower and the electric drill and had beaten all of them. On her own. She would not willingly become a helpless female again after tasting those victories.

This was, after all her home. She should have done the checking. Secretly though, she was glad she didn't have to, just this once. She carried the groceries into the kitchen and switched the lamps on in the lounge.

Polished hardwood floors gleamed in the warm light.

Comfortable sofas flanked an antique green tiled fireplace in the lounge room. A wide carved coffee table, one of Luke's, held pride of place, standing on a muted grey transitional rug that picked out the greens of the fireplace. In the centre of the coffee table, out of reach of tiny hands stood a crystal rose bowl that reflected the light into tiny rainbows.

One wall was adorned with a huge canvas of a perfect farmhouse, flanked by laden apple trees and a startling red maple that almost stole the show. On the wide front steps sat a man and woman with a small girl perched between them.

Ally glanced at them briefly, her eyes welling with sudden tears as she realized how close she had been to seeing her Mum and Dad again. She looked away quickly before the tears had a chance to fall. Automatically, she picked up several toys from the floor and put them away. One teddy looked at her sadly from the basket and she picked it up and held it close to her face. She could still smell Nicholas' baby scent on the bear. Her eyes prickled harder, where was he? She almost forgot Jim was there until she heard him move, He was standing near the door to the rest of the house. It was obvious that his search had proved fruitless.

"Please take a seat," she invited, "while I make something to eat."

"Would you like me to help?" Jim offered. The woman looked lost in her own home. She was clutching a bedraggled teddy bear as if it was her only friend in the world. He was afraid she was slipping into shock. If someone had stolen his child, he would probably be close to losing his sanity too. At times like these he was glad he had no one to lose.

"No thanks, I can manage." Ally needed to be alone with her thoughts. The kitchen was her favourite room. It shared the chimney with the lounge but here she had stripped it back to the original brick that contrasted with the bright Hamptons kitchen.

Nicholas' teddy stared solemnly at her and she looked back at him equally seriously. "Our Nicky is going to be OK," she whispered to the bear. "He has to be."

The bear said nothing.

Ally sat him on the counter and put the kettle on. While it was heating, she made sandwiches. She realised she hadn't eaten all day. Hunger was followed by a punch of guilt. Sighing, she traced the lines of Nicholas' latest finger painting hanging on the fridge before reaching for the milk bottle.

In the lounge, Jim relaxed on the sofa and thought how comfortable and lived in this room was. It reflected her style, beautiful, quiet, understated. He could feel the happiness that had filled it before tragedy had hit. Abruptly feeling like a traitor, he sat forward, frowning. He shouldn't be here. Feeling her eyes on him, he turned. Could she guess what he was thinking?

She was standing uncertainly in the doorway holding a tray and looking at him with a questioning gaze. But this time there was less mistrust in her wide green eyes. Good, he told himself, getting her to trust him was what his job entailed. He still felt uncomfortable though, sitting in her home.

Ally set the tray down and sat opposite him. The coffee table's presence seemed to echo the man who created it. It was a barrier between them, and not just a physical one.

They ate the simple meal in silence before Ally sat back to regard him steadily. He looked back at her calmly and she couldn't read anything in his eyes. He certainly was a cool customer, this Jim Conrad. Well, she would see if she could rattle him just a little.

"You can start explaining now," she said firmly.

"Would you believe that I was a simple bystander who saw what happened and wants to help?" he smiled, lifting his hands palms up. The submissive gesture was at odds with his character, she guessed.

"Not likely," she retorted. "You know way too much to be just a casual witness and you certainly aren't simple. You knew where I lived, before I even told you. But for some reason I do believe you want to help. I just don't know why."

Soberly he admitted, "I knew your husband."

"Knew Luke?" She flinched. Not what she expected. But it was possible. Luke's past was a mystery. There were so many things she did not know. She had never met any of his friends. Again, she cursed her ignorance, and his secrecy.

"Yes, we went to university in Sydney together. Don't tell me he never told you about the pranks we played on the lecturers?"

Ally felt she had been hit in the stomach. She had not even known that Luke had been to university. He had never mentioned it, or Jim Conrad. He'd certainly had plenty of opportunities. What had he studied? Why was he making furniture? She dared not betray her ignorance to Jim by asking what they had studied even though the questions burned in her mind. She would look it up tonight if the records were public.

"Go on," she urged shakily.

"We had lost touch over the years, then Luke rang me six weeks ago and asked me to fly up. He didn't give me any details but said his family's life was in danger and he needed my help. I arrived in Brisbane the next morning and found out he had been in an accident. "Damn!" he said, standing up abruptly and turning to the fireplace so she couldn't see his face. "I didn't do a very good job did I?"

"There wasn't much anyone could have done," Ally replied, feeling the need to reassure him, even though his story seemed a little forced. "It happened so fast. But why didn't you come and see us if you were Luke's friend? Why didn't you come to the funeral?"

"You didn't know me. I didn't want to scare you by showing up at your doorstep out of the blue. If I hadn't tried to keep out of your way, I could have stopped those men from taking your son."

"How long have you been following us?" Ally asked.

"Since Luke died. I just checked on you occasionally, you haven't been under surveillance." Jim was amazed at how easily the lies rolled off his tongue.

All those disturbing moments came flooding back. Many times, she had glanced over her shoulder, feeling eyes boring into her back, to find no one there. Each time she felt more frightened and exposed, whether it was on a train or a deserted dusty street, shimmering in the afternoon sun.

Now she found out that it was this man who had been responsible. How could he just sit there and admit it? Or was it? The eyes she had felt were malevolent, evil, surely not Jim Conrad's eyes. She didn't intend to let him off the hook so easily though.

"I don't like being spied on," she said mustering some coldness.

"And I'm sorry," Jim returned softly, hoping she wouldn't notice his slight hesitation before launching into a lie, "but I did promise Luke, and after he died, I felt I had to do what he wanted. I'm angry at myself for not talking to you instead. Of being worried about your reaction. It was easier, but it was stupid.

Seeing how furious Jim was with himself, Ally's own anger dissolved. This thoughtfulness, even though it had frightened her at the time, was welcome. He was right, she probably would not have wanted a stranger appearing at Luke's funeral, wanting to look after her. Her pain had been too raw. She found comfort only in Nicholas. Nicky where are you? Ally changed the subject to stop herself screaming.

"Are you a private investigator?" she asked.

"Not exactly. I'm a freelance corporate trouble-shooter."

"And what is a trouble-shooter?" This wasn't an occupation Ally had ever heard of, it sounded like something out of an old western. Unbidden, a picture of him in dusty Levi's and a weather-beaten Stetson riding into town on his horse armed to the teeth came to mind. The image suited him perfectly, a trouble shooter. Ally turned away, hiding a smile. Luckily, he didn't notice her lapse in concentration for he answered her question quite seriously.

"I'm hired by companies to find out why they aren't thriving. I check the books, the personnel, the operation. Sometimes even if I can't find anything illegal going on, I can find areas of waste, like the fourteen luxury company cars that were being used out of work hours in the last job I did."

"It sounds like an interesting job," Ally said.

"It's a pretty good living. I get to travel and live in the lap of luxury sometimes but there is a lot of tedious paperwork and investigation of computer records looking for fraud and misappropriation of funds. You'd be surprised at how much money disappears."

"But you can't be terribly popular with the employees you investigate."

He grinned. "If they haven't done anything wrong, they generally don't have too much to worry about. I find positive encouragement and acknowledgement of their efforts and maybe some movie tickets or a hamper work way better than threats. But I love the puzzle of the investigation most. Finding industrial spies. People without scruples that sell out their workmates and their company for money. It's always rewarding to bring them to justice.

It's what I miss..." he stopped himself and grinned, "I'm talking too much about myself. Tell me a little about your work."

"It's nowhere as high powered as yours," Ally replied. "Louise and I started our own business from scratch after college. We worked from the apartment that we shared. At first, we had a few friends as our only clients, then word spread. After about two years we opened up a store that acts as our offices and showroom. Our specialty is a beachy Australian take on the Hamptons, the two styles come together so naturally."

"Judging by this room, I can understand why," Jim said appreciatively.

"Thank you! But this room is definitely more Canadian country than beachy", she smiled. "Anyway, we design interiors for show homes, apartments, offices and even one small mall, but mainly family homes. Some of our clients just want one statement piece, or a cushion, while others have an empty house and an open cheque book. Every day is different and I absolutely love it."

Jim thought about his apartment and how different it would look with Ally's touch. He smiled to himself as he continued to listen to her.

Her face lit up with enthusiasm as she spoke, "I always bring Nicholas into work with me. He is such a pleasure to have around." The vitality drained from her face leaving her bleak and frightened. Just for a little while she had been able to push the present out of her mind but now it was back in force and there was not one thing, she could do about it. She twisted her hands in her lap and silence spread until, with a jerky movement, Ally stood up.

"I think we should turn in now," she said tonelessly. "The guestroom is down the hall on the right. I'll keep my phone close."

Jim wanted to go to her, to comfort her, but he held himself back. Getting involved during a case would bring nothing but disaster. The last time he had trusted a beautiful woman, she had tried to manipulate him into looking the other way while she escaped to the Cayman's and her beloved bank account. It taught him that business and pleasure didn't mix.

A small voice in his head told him that if he became involved with Alexandria Reed, he wouldn't be as unscathed at the end of it. She wasn't a manipulator. She was a decent, honest person. Goodness shone out of her. Even in grief, when people reveal their worst side, she was nothing but good. He felt drawn to her despite himself. She was a widow, for heaven's sake! He had to leave her alone. So, he sat still and watched her walk away from him. It was the best way.

Ally tiptoed into the nursery and switched the light on. The signs of their hasty departure were evident everywhere. A cupboard hung open and baby clothes trailed out of it. The sky-blue quilt with happy teddies playing over its surface had been flung over the cot rails. Ally could almost feel Nicholas, sleepy and cuddly as she picked him up this morning, only hours ago.

Ally folded the clothes and made the cot as her hands tingled with the need to hold him again. After looking around at the now ordered and neat room she flicked the light off. Alone in her room she slumped on the bed. There was a lump in her throat so huge she could hardly swallow and her chest burned. Her eyelids were swollen with unshed tears. All day she had been doing something, anything to stop herself thinking that she might never see Nicholas again, never tuck him in, never play with him or comfort him. Never watch him grow up.

She considered contacting the enigmatic Max Reed but instantly dismissed the idea. He would deny any involvement in the kidnapping and would work swiftly to cover his tracks. Nicholas might be hurt in the process. No, she had to wait, and hope. Ally had never found waiting easy, but nothing she had ever experienced could compare to this. It was an intractable pain that she could not reach, could not touch.

Taking a deep shuddering breath Ally stood up and walked to the mirror. A distraught stranger looked back at her. Her usually neat hair was curling madly, and a rapidly darkening bruise contrasted with a chalk white complexion. Desperately frightened green eyes stared back at her.

"Oh God!" she said to herself. "I'm falling apart. I must be strong for Nicky. If he sees me like this, he won't even recognise me."

Quickly, she threw together her nightclothes and went to the bathroom where she stood under a stinging hot shower. She could barely feel the heat. She bent her head under the spray as the tears came. The more she tried to stop, the harder they fell until she just gave up and sobbed.

Finally, hiccupping and scrubbing her reddened nose on her wrist, she made herself calm down. Crying wouldn't help. She thought about the man in the other room. She was sure he would never cry.

Jim Conrad was a puzzle, the way he had just appeared at her side. And his story about keeping an eye out for her as a favour to Luke seemed a little too good to be true. Just as she needed a knight in shining armour, he had materialized. But if he was lying... Ally shuddered at the thought, then he could be one of Max Reed's hired guns. Letting him into her home might have been the greatest mistake she had ever made.

No, somehow, despite her doubts, she trusted him. His presence consoled her in an inexplicable way, even though he had not done anything overtly comforting, he had stayed with her. He had listened to her and made small talk, and made her feel less alone. Ally regretted again how secretive her husband had been about his past. Ignorance made her vulnerable. She didn't even know any of his friends. She didn't have a single photograph of him before they met. She didn't know where he grew up, or where he went to school. She hadn't known he had been to university and she didn't know if Jim was who he said he was. Was he married? Was there a wife or girlfriend waiting for him while he slept in Ally's spare room? He hadn't mentioned anyone and he had a lonely look that his self-confidence couldn't quite hide. When you had children, that look disappeared forever. What if you lost a child? Ally had always avoided thinking about that but she guessed the pain would never go away. She prayed she would never find out.

Taking a deep breath, she turned the shower off and dried herself on a fluffy white towel in her gleaming bathroom. Dressing in soft, cotton pyjamas, she walked slowly back into her room. There was a lock on her door, but she didn't use it. She felt safe. The crisp linen sheets for once didn't welcome her. Finally, after tossing for what seemed like hours, her brain became so exhausted from running endless scenarios that filled her head with a maze of terrifying possibilities that it let her drift off into an uneasy slumber.

Jim waited patiently until Ally had stopped moving before leaving his room. His bare feet made no sound on the polished wood floor of the corridor.

He walked into the lounge room where he carefully unscrewed the backplate of the landline and removed the listening device that he installed several weeks ago. It had served its purpose, allowing him to be at the airport this morning. It was a pity he wasn't in time to stop those two thugs from snatching the little boy. Max Reed was a control freak who just had to have more than one scheme going at once and Jim was quietly furious that his old friend's brother had interfered with his careful plans. He could not even guess at the man's motives.

Max had hired Jim to keep an eye on Ally and Nicky, hinting at some unspecified danger, then had tied Jim's hands behind his back, ordering him to stay well clear of the pair. Why the abduction then? A test of his ability, or another way of protecting the boy. Those two at the airport worried him. The business suits may have disguised their innate stupidity to most people but Jim knew the type. In time, and he would stake his reputation on it, they would make a mistake and give themselves away.

He hoped it would be soon because they'd be lousy babysitters. Thinking about them Jim began to wonder how they knew about the airport. Surely not another bug?

He quietly began checking. Fortunately, the moon had risen, bathing the room in silvery light. It was a restful room and he wished he could have seen it under different circumstances.

Since he had opened a door on her life, Jim had not been able to get Alexandria Reed out of his head. Even when he wasn't watching over her, she invaded his every waking thought. Hell, she invaded his dreams.

Now he had walked through that door and had become part of her life. He had looked right into her green eyes. He had even felt the fine small bones of her arm through her cool, soft skin. This small taste of her presence made him so hungry for more that it hurt.

Family snapshots lining the walls of the hall showed a beautiful young woman with clouds of light brown hair and a dazzling smile. While Jim searched the room, he tried to remember if he'd ever seen her smile like that, during the time he'd had her under surveillance. He hadn't. Hopefully once this was over, she could rebuild her life with the child and get that smile back. Fleetingly he imagined being part of that future. Who was he kidding? Ally would hate his guts if, or rather when, she found out his true intent. As for the future, he needed no one in his. And then, there was Luke, sandy haired and serious. Jim felt a sharp pang of pity when he thought of the dead man. Silently, he pledged to look after his family.

About the size and colour of a fly, a spy-cam was sitting on the bookshelf with a clear view of the fireplace and the seats flanking it. Jim picked it up with his thumb over the iris and turned it over. Small, expensive, state of the art. Damn shame, he thought as it swirled down the toilet but too dangerous to leave lying around. Sooner or later the cops would search this house and he didn't want them stumbling onto anything that could complicate things.

His work finished, Jim went back to the guest room and prepared for bed. His constant companion, a .45 semi-automatic made a comforting bulge under the pillow. The last image he saw before he fell asleep was of a younger happier Alexandria smiling down at him.

Chapter Two

Brisbane

Ally sleepily rolled over and opened her eyes. The house was silent. She couldn't remember the last time she had wakened before Nicholas. By now he should be calling her from his cot or crying...with a start she woke up and remembered. She sat bolt upright, heart thudding. Guilt and anguish stabbed through her. She had forgotten. How could she? How could she have slept, without her baby safe beside her? Not a single call all night. No one had found him. No one had demanded a ransom. She held her phone, willing it to ring.

Fear and desolation flooded in. He was gone, who knows where and with whom. Someone else was touching her baby. Feeding him, bathing him, changing his nappies. Oh, please don't let them hurt him, she prayed. She couldn't go on. She couldn't get out of bed. Her legs wouldn't hold her up.

No, don't give up. Determinedly she put a clamp on her emotions and swung her legs over the side of the bed. She moved heavily, trying to keep going. She had a lot of work to do to get her baby back. The press conference was this morning. Ally had to get ready, it was vital that she be there to tell people what had happened, maybe someone watching the news had seen those two men and where they had gone.

Pulling some tailored pants and a silk blouse from her cupboard, Ally made her way to her bathroom. Her face was a mess, the ugly bruise pulling her cheek out of shape and dark shadows framed her eyes.

Gingerly, she applied concealer and foundation over the bruise. It was too dark to hide completely, but it looked better. After a tawny blush and neutral lipstick, she looked almost human, even though she still felt like death.

The wavy hair flowing down her back merited just a quick brush. The days of careful hairstyles were over. Luke had loved her long hair and when Nicholas tangled his little fingers in it Ally was barely able to handle the memories.

The smell of coffee drew her to the kitchen. Jim was sitting at the island. Two mugs of coffee sat in front of him, steam curling up into the sunshine that streamed in through the windows. The teddy bear hadn't moved. He still sat forlornly in the sunshine looking as lonely and miserable as only an abandoned toy can. Ally blinked back tears.

Watching Jim for a moment before he noticed her, Ally realised that she was very glad that he was there. If it wasn't for him, she would be totally and completely alone now. Jim looked up before she had even completed the thought. She wasn't ready for his eyes. She felt like she had been walking a tightrope, and a sudden gust of wind had blown her off balance. What was it about this man that affected her equilibrium so much?

"Good morning," he smiled. "I heard you moving around so I took the liberty of making coffee. How do you have yours?"

"Hello, um, just a little milk, thanks," Ally answered flushing. Jim filled her kitchen with a strong masculine presence. His broad shoulders and powerful chest were enhanced by the cotton sweater he wore over faded jeans. The sleeves of the sweater were pushed up, revealing tanned, well-muscled forearms. She met his eyes again, momentarily mesmerised by their grey depths before looking away slightly breathless. Damn girl, she thought. Get a grip.

"I see you've found our best kept secret," she gestured to the mound of pastries nestling in paper in the middle of the quartz topped island.

"You have an excellent bakery," Jim replied, "I didn't know what you like, so I bought one of everything."

"You'd better take care, these things are lethal for your waistline," Ally smiled as she took a pecan Danish from the delectable assortment.

"You have nothing to worry about in that department," Jim let the compliment escape his lips. The loose cut of her blouse could not quite hide her narrow waist and gently rounded breasts.

"Why thank you," Ally smiled with a touch of embarrassment, remembering her scrawny teenage years. After a fairly normal childhood, she had suddenly shot up to her full height one summer, way before the other kids in her class. It had been an awkward and traumatic time. She had felt clumsy and unattractive and in the depths of her mind that girl still existed.

Jim noticed how one of her eyebrows curved higher than the other when she smiled giving her a slightly lopsided look that only added to her beauty. The simple cut of her hair emphasised the clean lines of her features – the high cheekbones, the full mouth, those incredible green eyes. The smile didn't quite reach those eyes which were shuttered with habitual sadness. His eyes settled on the ugly bruise and evidence of the violence that she had endured. Anger stirred.

They ate in silence while the spectre of the kidnappers hovered around them. After breakfast, Jim switched on the television in the plant filled nook that adjoined the kitchen while Ally tidied up. The morning show was on and the hosts were making sympathetic noises. Nicholas' name and snatches of conversation travelled into the kitchen. "...devastating...no new leads...possible tragedy..."

The mug Ally had been rinsing clattered from her fingers as she grabbed the sink for support, she was so cold. Jim was behind her in an instant, holding her up. Blindly she turned towards him. Enveloped in his soft sweater, she shook with fear and grief. Why did they say tragedy? They must know something. Hearing the words aloud made it all the more real. This was worse than any nightmare.

Slowly the warmth of Jim's body seeped across to her and she stopped shivering. His chest against her cheek felt as solid as a rock wall. and she could hear his heart thudding slowly, calmly. With an illogical certainty, she knew that this man would protect her and find her baby. She had been so independent during these past months, with no one but herself to count on, that the relief at being able to lean on someone else was immense. She felt her muscles relax and let go as the tension drained out of her.

Jim held Ally tightly, waiting for the trembling to stop. He hated those thugs for doing this to an innocent mother and child, hated Max Reed for putting her in the firing line and hated himself for being part of this mess. She felt small and fragile in his arms like an injured bird. Her soft hair tickled his chin. Up close he could see that some of the strands were shot through with pure gold. Despite himself, he bent his head to breathe in her fragrance. She smelled nice... like fresh flowers maybe. He imagined Ally sitting in a garden full of pink roses with the sun glinting off her hair. She laughed, waiting for him to join her.

Annoyed with himself for daydreaming about things that could never be, Jim cleared his throat and said more harshly than he meant to, "We should get going if we're to get to your press conference in time."

"Yes...yes of course," Ally stammered, flushing as she moved out of the safety of his arms. What must he be thinking of her, clinging to him like that?

Gathering her bag and jacket, she quickly followed him downstairs to the car. They drove into the city centre while the spring warmth intensified. Neither was comfortable enough to start a conversation, even about the weather. Ally made an effort to casually look out of the window, the rapport they felt earlier had deserted them.

Jim left Ally at Police Headquarters on Masterton saying he had some business to take care of. She had a niggling feeling that the blue uniforms made him uncomfortable but she told herself it was just her imagination.

Donna Marshal, the federal policewoman Ally had met at the airport was waiting for her at the front desk.

"Have the kidnappers contacted you?" she asked quietly.

"No. Not a word."

Donna frowned. "No witnesses have come forward as yet. We are hoping the press conference will produce some new leads." She led Ally into the press room. A low table at one end faced rows of hardbacked chairs where several reporters were already encamped, murmuring.

A hush fell over the room and Ally felt all eyes on her. Donna touched her arm reassuringly and showed her to the centre seat at the table. Facing a dozen fluffy microphones, she had a hysterical desire to giggle at how silly they looked before the grim reality of the situation reasserted itself. Resolutely, she looked over them to the reporters.

Donna introduced Ally and urged her to recount the events leading up to and including the kidnapping. She started to, faltered, tried again. Hesitantly, she explained how she was held by one man, while the other took Nicholas. She gave a description of the two kidnappers. Tears flooded her eyes as she described Nicky and asked for help in finding him. The policewoman took over, showing a large photo of Nicholas, detailing the nationwide search and urging the public to come forward with any information.

Ally spent an hour after the conference unsuccessfully looking at mugshots before emerging exhausted out of the building and into the bright September sunshine.

Jim sat on the steps eating hot chips out of a paper bag. Taking one look at her, he grinned sympathetically and handed her the bag. Digging in, she encountered a wet mess.

"Ugh," she said withdrawing a soggy chip, "you've got gravy on these!"

"Best way to eat them," Jim laughed.

"Nicky loves chips with gravy," Ally replied wistfully.

"The kid has good taste then. We'll buy him some soon."

"And I bet I'll have to wipe both your faces," Ally complained as she took out a tissue and wiped a slight trace of gravy from the corner of Jim's firm mouth. She tried not to notice his indrawn breath as she touched him and the way he suddenly stilled. His eyes were fastened on hers with an unreadable expression.

"I think I would gladly clean a million gallons of gravy just to see him again." Ally knew that she was talking too fast, but she couldn't help herself.

"You will see him, Ally. Now eat up. You don't think I'm going to let you in the Stang eating gravy, do you?"

Ally was secretly relieved at how he lightened the moment. The quick change from intense to playful was obviously designed to make her feel better and she was grateful at his thoughtfulness.

When they got home, they found Charlie, Ally's neighbour sitting on the front steps. He rose slowly to greet her, his kind face crinkled with concern.

"Charlie!" Ally exclaimed. "When did you get back from your holiday?"

"As soon as I heard about our little Nicholas. Has there been any news?" He was so sympathetic that she almost dissolved in tears.

"No, there's not Charlie but the police are doing everything they can."

"Can I help?"

"No, not really," Ally replied, "we just have to wait."

At this moment, Charlie seemed to notice the other man standing behind Ally with his hands in his pockets, looking casually disinterested. Since Luke's death, he had been very helpful and protective of her and Nicky. He frowned as Ally introduced him to Jim. As the two men shook hands, Ally glanced at Jim and was surprised to see a brief flash of strong emotion that chased across his features before the indifferent expression settled there once more.

"Come in for lunch Charlie," Ally invited, sensing an undercurrent in the silence, but Charlie declined, saying he had already eaten and was ready for a nap. Limping away, he again offered his help.

The house felt empty and dark. This was only the second time since he had been born that Ally was home without Nicholas. His absence echoed hollowly off the hardwood floors. She silently prepared a simple salad for lunch, helped by Jim, who, as if understanding her need for peace, didn't speak. They ate in front of the TV. The leading story of the five-minute hourly news update was about Nicholas' abduction. Ally was amazed and grateful for the coverage. The search for Nicky had captured the imagination of the entire state. A brief segment showed her impassioned plea at the news conference this morning. Ally could barely recognise the anguished woman on the screen and in a surreal moment felt for her. A few shots of internet sensationalist theories rounded out the 30 second spot. She hoped it was enough.

Jim's heart tore as he watched her. Unable to help himself, he closed the distance between them and hugged her tightly. "Those animals who took your baby and hurt you are going to pay. I'll make sure they do."

Ally's heart skipped a beat as she heard the raw emotion in his voice and she looked up at him. Their eyes locked. A feeling she had thought was dead forever stirred deep inside her. She didn't move for a second as her mobile rang in her pocket. She blinked, breaking the spell, then answered it. It was Donna. The crime lab people were on their way to search the house for any possible evidence, as well as a fingerprint expert, computer tech and photographer.

"Crime lab?" Ally asked.

"Don't worry Mrs Reed. They are part of our team because of their thoroughness. Whereas the computer guy will check the files, they will dismantle the laptop itself and put it back together. They will check every jam jar, every rafter. If there is evidence related to the kidnapping, they'll find it." Donna sounded quietly confident.

"I hope they do. How long will it take?"

"It may take an entire day to complete but we have included a few constables to check the exterior, so I estimate only four or five hours. I'd like you to stay and assist in the investigation if that's convenient."

"Of course! I can't think of anything but Nicholas." Feeling Jim standing beside her, she knew, deep in her heart that there was something else she was unwillingly focusing on. Something very special and something she hoped would still be there when this nightmare was over.

A team of plain clothed officers arrived within minutes of the call and set to work with quiet efficiency. Ally and Jim stayed out of the way, leaning on the back veranda railing, staring at the wide, lazy river below. Sparks of sunlight reflected off the tiny wavelets whipped up by a sneaky spring breeze. A ferry moved slowly across the river, leaving a wake of muddy water. Fairy Martins flew like miniature fighter jets, swooping inches from the water's surface, catching insects in mid-flight.

"Pollution has to be a problem with all those industrial estates upstream." Jim commented.

"The local government comes down very strongly on offenders," Ally smiled, "but the colour is off putting. They dredge the river all the time but it doesn't help enough. Did you know that even hundreds of years ago when Captain Cook was sailing up the east coast, he predicted a large river by the amount of mud in the ocean they were crossing? There's a lovely park down near the river, with heaps of play equipment."

The smile left her face and Jim saw her withdraw into her own private hell. He kept talking softly but he knew she no longer heard him.

The police left mid-afternoon. Ally breathed a sigh of relief as their cars pulled out and drove away. There had been so many of them and they just keep going through her things. The invasion, though necessary and legal, was still confronting.

Wearily, she shut the front door and leaned her forehead on it. The phone rang. Her heart jumped. She rummaged in her pocket to answer it. Private number.

"Hello?" she said breathlessly.

Nothing. Just a hollow sound, a silent echo of a raindrop in a deserted forest.

"Hello... is there anyone there?" Ally felt fear creep into her voice and clamped her teeth together to stop them chattering.

The silence continued for long seconds then a distinct click severed the connection and a dull beeping tone followed.

Ally felt Jim behind her. She turned to face his questioning gaze.

"It sounded like no one was there, but there was. They hung up deliberately without saying anything."

"If it rings again, let me answer it."

They didn't have long to wait. Jim let the phone ring three agonizing times, before pressing accept. He listened, not bothering to speak. Shrugging as he hung up, he thought maybe it was some sick joker who had seen the news and liked playing tricks on vulnerable women.

The phone rang again. This time he answered instantly and unleashed a barrage of swear words, calling the unknown person on the other end of the line a spineless coward in no uncertain terms. His normally rumbly voice was a harsh growl.

Ally was surprised to say the least, especially when Jim turned to her, completely calm, with a quiet controlled voice.

"Sorry about that bit of prose. If it was some weirdo who wanted to scare you because he thinks you're alone, he won't ring again."

The phone rang three more times that afternoon, Ally frayed nerves were stretching to breaking point. She felt sick and dizzy. Donna confirmed that the trace on her mobile could not pin point the caller's location.

Jim broke into her thoughts, "Do you have anything to let you relax?"

"My doctor prescribed medications after Luke, but I threw them out. I needed my wits to look after Nicky. He was such a tiny baby then. He'd wake up so many times in the middle of the night. Even without drugs I'd stumble about like a zombie, but with the sedatives I couldn't open my eyes and fell asleep in the chair with him on my lap and only woke up when he started rolling down to my feet."

"How about a scotch then?"

"That I do have," Ally smiled tiredly, "for special occasions. Will you join me? I hate to drink alone."

"Yeah, I might at that. It's been a hell of a day." Jim poured the whiskey into some cut crystal glasses. It was a single malt Louise had picked up in Scotland during a buying trip. The fiery liquid comforted as it travelled down past her throat. She found herself accepting a second glass and started to feel warmer and more relaxed. She snuggled into the sofa, grateful for its softness.

When Jim excused himself to get clothes from his apartment, Ally barely noticed as she drifted into slumber.

She would have been horrified to see him drive his car only a few hundred metres into the underground carpark of the high-rise apartment block overlooking her street.

He entered cautiously, always alert. Even when he was sure his bare rooms were secure, he didn't turn the lights on, but sat in front of the full-length windows listening to the silence and watching the sunset washing over the western sky. Ally's house was quiet below him, the curtains drawn. He didn't expect to see her.

The phone purred softly beside him. "I had the situation under control before your goons blew it. You are paying me some serious money to work on this case exclusively. I'm letting other contracts slide to watch your sister-in-law. If you just wanted some idiot to jerk around, why pick me? What the hell are you thinking?" Jim felt rage bubbling inside him and forced himself to calm down.

The rich baritone on the other end replied, "I had nothing to do with it!"

Jim let his silent disbelief travel down the line.

"What you believe is irrelevant. I anticipated that Alexandria and my nephew would become targets. That is why I hired you, not some idiot. You failed to protect them."

Jim knew that better than anyone but he wasn't ready to concede just yet. "There was no way I could have been close enough with the ridiculous restrictions you had put on me."

Max Reed had no time for recriminations. "The question is, what are you doing to rectify the situation?"

Something about the even tone reached Jim. "They weren't your men?" he asked quietly.

"No Conrad. I hired you to look after my sister-in-law and her son. Not to harm them."

"What about the calls?"

"Now what are you accusing me of?" The man on the other end of the line was getting angry, hardly the response Jim would have expected.

Fear uncoiled in Jim's stomach. If it was true that Max Reed wasn't responsible for the kidnapping then Nicholas was in even greater danger and he had no leads. He was an idiot not to have considered the possibility before. All this time he had been sitting around, playing the concerned friend role, when he should have been doing his job. Investigating. Max was still waiting for a reply.

"Ally needed help at the airport, so I offered my assistance. I am staying at her house, so I can protect her if they try anything else, and to be on hand if there is any word from the kidnappers. Someone has been harassing her on the phone. It didn't seem your style though."

"Thanks a lot, Conrad. Your faith in me is remarkable." Max sounded only a little sarcastic and didn't take offence for which Jim was grateful. Even though he was not afraid of the man, the way many people were, he didn't relish having Max Reed as an enemy. The man was too powerful. He was the complete opposite of his late brother Luke, who was content to make furniture in a tiny workshop and have long lunches with his wife. Max never had lunch unless it was a business meeting and spent most of his time growing his millions.

Which just proved that money and power didn't necessarily guarantee happiness. Of the two brothers, Luke had more of the things that really mattered. A million dollars did not compare with Ally's fleeting smile. Shaking off the thought, Jim completed his report and ended the call quickly. He then rang a PI he worked with closely and gave him concise instructions. The investigation would begin tonight. He had to get back to Ally, she could also be in danger.

Ally woke to the sound of the phone ringing in her ear. The bed was singularly uncomfortable today. Lifting her head, she groaned as pain shot through her neck and forehead. She had been lying face down on the sofa with a pillow jammed against the bruise on the side of her head.

"Oh, shut up!" Ally said to the phone. Her tongue felt too big for her mouth, and her words slurred together. "I'm not getting up again." Nevertheless, she answered it groggily, her head hurt and she vowed not to use alcohol as an analgesic again.

"Hello?" she asked the hollow sound, not really expecting an answer.

"Are you alone?" a crackling metallic voice rasped.

It might have been male or female. The voice was being digitally altered to sound like a menacing robot.

"Yes," Ally whispered, instantly awake and sober.

"Do you want to see your son again?"

"Yes, yes please tell me if he's all right. Please don't hurt him." Did she really sound as shaky and pathetic as that?

"Listen closely." The voice ordered with no change in tone. "The flower carnival in Toowoomba, do you know it?"

"Yes," Ally responded, confused. Of all the things she expected to hear it wasn't that. It was September, so Toowoomba, a mountain city about an hour and a half out of Brisbane would be celebrating the coming of spring with street parades, gardens festooned with flowers and fireworks. She hadn't even thought about going this year, her life was so full of darkness. "I think so..." she stammered.

"Go to the Ferris wheel in the park. Tomorrow. Noon. There will be a letter for you at the ticket booth. When you get to the top of the Ferris wheel, open the letter. Come alone. If you bring the boyfriend the deal is off."

"But my son..."

The phone was dead. Ally held the handpiece as if it would bring the caller back. It was her only link to Nicholas. Should she ring Donna and ask if the call could be traced? Ally knew from tv shows that the time was too short. And the caller had waited until she was alone. That meant they were watching her. If they didn't want Jim involved, then calling the police would put Nicky in even more danger.

No, this was something she would have to do herself. She would find out what the kidnappers' demands were and she would give then anything they asked for. She would let them take her soul to get her baby back.

She had to find a car. Louise's car was still at the airport. Her partner would need it when she returned from Europe in a few days. No, she had to hire a car. Suddenly Ally remembered Charlie. He had a little compact car that he hardly used.

The sound of the door opening made her jump. It was Jim coming back with his clothes. He mustn't suspect anything. She had to go alone. If he knew her secret, he would insist on helping and that couldn't happen. Nicky's life depended on it.

He was frowning when he came in. "What is it?" she breathed when she saw his face. "Is it Nicholas? Have they..."

"No, I haven't heard anything." There hadn't been a ransom demand either which was bad. Jim hid his concern. "I was just a bit worried about leaving you alone. Let's sit down. I need to ask you a few questions.

"What do you want to know?" Ally asked facing him across the coffee table.

"Tell me about Luke's accident." Jim said hating himself for causing the sudden look of anguish that appeared on Ally's already grief-stricken face.

"Oh, it was so pointless, Jim," she almost whispered. "He usually drove a work truck to auctions and demolition sites for materials – doors, beams, fireplaces. That day, it was a Thursday morning, the truck wouldn't start, so he took my little car." She paused for a long time, imagining what happened next.

"Where was he going?" Jim prompted.

"To an auction just over the border on the Tweed Coast. Anyway, it was midmorning on a clear day, light traffic..." Ally's face took on that faraway look again, as if she was reliving the scene. "A truck came across three lanes of traffic and ploughed right into him. He didn't have a chance in my little car. If it had been the bigger vehicle...maybe he would have had a chance. He was so beautiful and loving and talented." her voice choked with tears. Even now, this was unbearable. This pain. And every time she thought of Luke, she tried to remember him happy, kind, funny. And instead, her mind took her down that dim hallway in the hospital morgue. No matter how hard she fought it, she would end up near the broken, shrouded figure. And the sheet would be lifted and she would see Luke's face, white, lifeless, never to smile again. Then having hurt her enough, her mind would let her tear away and think of something else. She lifted her head and blinked. Jim was looking at her with concern. She pulled herself back to the present. The accident. She went on, "the car was crushed and ended up in an embankment."

"What about the truck driver?"

"It didn't stop, and there were no tyre marks that would have been left if the driver had tried to brake. The witnesses said it looked deliberate." Ally stopped short of telling him that her mechanic had found that the truck had been immobilized, possibly deliberately, too. "Why do you want to know? Do you think there's a connection?"

"Do you?" Jim countered.

Ally faced a dilemma. She had told no one of her suspicions. Afraid that she and Nicky would be next. But she had to trust someone, and for some unfathomable reason she trusted Jim. She had invited him, a total stranger into her home. She had slept in the room next to him without fear and he made her feel safe.

Taking a deep breath, she blurted, "I think that both my husband and my son have been taken from me by the same man. Max Reed, Luke's older brother. I have never met him, but I know he's capable of anything."

An hour ago, Jim would have agreed with her, but after his conversation with Max, he had serious doubts. "Why?"

"There was no love lost between the two brothers. You see," she paused, "he blamed Luke for the death of his pregnant wife."

"What?" Jim exclaimed, shocked. This was something he knew nothing about. How could he not know this?

"Ironically it was a car accident. Katie went into labour and Luke was the only one there. His car skidded out of control in heavy rain and hit a tree. Luke said the steering just broke. Katie had stopped breathing but they kept her on a ventilator long enough to deliver the baby. It was a boy. He lived long enough for Max to see him and hold him and fall in love with him. And then he died too."

"I could see how he would be bitter."

There was a long silence before Ally resumed. "To my knowledge, they never spoke again. Luke had broken ribs and pelvis. After he was released from hospital he travelled north."

"What a tragedy. Max lost a brother as well."

"Luke never talked about it," Ally continued quietly, "until the anniversary of their deaths. And never afterwards, but I knew he thought about it all the time. I was hoping that our life together would heal the old wounds and they would reconnect, but there was no time."

"When I spoke with Luke, he mentioned threats." How much longer could he keep lying to her?

"They began soon after Nicholas was born. We were so happy. The messages were so vague. Luke said they were just crank calls and told me not to worry. I didn't at first until I overheard one. Luke admitted he knew it was Max even though the voice was digital." It took all of her will power not to tell him of the phone call she had just received. She hated deceiving him. Only for Nicholas would she do this. She had to get away from his intense grey eyes before she broke down and told him everything.

"Excuse me," she stood up abruptly. "The news will be on."

The press conference had been condensed to thirty seconds of prime time and the newsreader concluded by saying that the police were following up leads. Ally sat slumped in front of the television, looking up any snippets of online news she could find until Jim switched it off. He wanted to reach out to her but stopped himself. The only thing that would help would be to get her son back. And despite his reassurances, he knew that the longer there was no word from the kidnappers, the more chance there was that Nicholas may already be dead. Some parents never found out the fate of their children. They existed in a living hell for years, always searching. It was the worst thing he could image and he hoped that the future held something kinder for Ally.

Chapter Three

Toowoomba

Only a small bag, one that Jim wouldn't notice. She packed nothing for herself, only a change of clothes, nappies and formula. It made her feel better thinking she might be bringing Nicholas home today.

She went to bed again, but sleep wouldn't come. Her heart pounded as she made up stories to tell Jim about taking a trip alone. None of them sounded even remotely plausible, even to her. Giving up, she pulled on a pair of jeans, a pale mauve t-shirt, running shoes and a quilted jacket. She had decided to tell him she was going to visit some old friends.

When she finally went into the kitchen, she found a note from Jim lying on the counter. He would be back in the afternoon. Something he had to do urgently. Ally breathed a sigh of relief. She didn't have to lie after all.

Charlie was happy to lend her his car. "The poor thing needs a run just to keep the engine from seizing up like its owner," he laughed making her a cup of tea.

"Oh Charlie, you're not old!"

She hugged him when she left. "You are such a dear friend. I can always count on you. Thank you so much."

"My pleasure, dear. Take care on those roads. Where did you say you were going anyway?"

"I didn't Charlie. It's better that I don't."

"Is it about our Nicky?"

"I'm sorry Charlie."

"Yes, yes, I understand. It is better if I don't know. Be careful. If you need any help, call me. I am going to stay with my daughter for a few days but I can drop everything, any time. Do you have her number? Mobile reception is bad out there. And please call me if you have any news."

"I will, I promise. Thanks again."

After waving goodbye, she set off for Toowoomba. Soon she had left the sprawling, busy city and headed into the open country of the Lockyer Valley. Tidy rows of vegetables interspersed with green paddocks of grazing cattle spread out on either side of the highway.

Ally barely noted the rural scenery though. Her hands were cramping from holding the steering wheel too tightly and her neck ached from scanning the rear-view mirror. There it was again. Far behind her, so she only caught glimpses of it now and then on long straights. The glint of sunshine off the bonnet of a white car. It was staying a respectable distance behind her, even when faster cars came between them and passed them in turn, the other car did not speed up. It did not completely disappear either.

Ally told herself it was just a coincidence that it was travelling at exactly the same speed as she was, that it slowed down and sped up just when she did. It didn't help. Finally, she gave up wondering and turned off at a service station. She still had a lot of time and she needed to rest and calm down. It was just after ten. Two hours until she had to be at the Ferris wheel. Shading her eyes, she peered into the distance. Toowoomba was already visible, nestling high above the plains in the blue hills of the Great Dividing Range.

The white car turned out to be an early model Japanese car. Hardly a vehicle to inspire fear. It sped past her on the highway, the two male occupants not sparing her so much as a glance.

Ally parked the car and walked in. A small diner was attached to the service station and she ordered a strong coffee to keep her going and a cheesecake to settle her nerves. "Stop being paranoid!" she told herself. Just because she was going to a strange city to read a letter from a kidnapper on top of a Ferris wheel at high noon didn't mean that the rest of the world was following her.

"Pardon?" the waitress had stopped at her table and Ally realised she was talking to herself.

"I was just saying this is a great cheesecake," she mumbled through a mouthful of crumbs.

"Would you like me to bring you another slice?" the waitress asked.

"Would love it but no, my scales wouldn't approve!"

"I know exactly what you mean," the waitress laughed patting her own hip.

Ally laughed with her, savouring the female kinship she felt with this woman she would probably never see again. It felt so normal for a second, to be worrying about her weight. Then she stopped laughing. It was time to be on the road again.

But what was at the end of the road?

The car responded smoothly as she guided it out onto the highway between long chains of cars in both lanes. There was no shortage of people travelling up to Toowoomba today it seemed. Ally settled in for a slow drive. She was glad she had left early because she was so tired and tense. Turning on the radio, she relaxed a little as the sweet strains of a love song filled the car.

Ahead, on the shoulder of the road, something white shimmered. As she drew nearer, she saw that it was the old white car. Its indicator flashed as she passed it and it pulled out aggressively into the stream of traffic two cars behind her. Ally felt a gathering tightness in her chest as her heart sped up with a surge of adrenalin. She felt completely awake and terribly afraid. Fumbling, she turned the radio off. A quick glance in the rear-view mirror told her that the white car was content to keep two cars between them. She was trapped with nowhere to run. Momentarily, Ally thought of turning onto a side road, but rejected the idea almost immediately. On a lonely backroad they could force her off the road any time they wanted with no witnesses. And she had to be in Toowoomba at noon, no matter what. The letter could be telling her where Nicholas was waiting for her.

The needle crept up slightly and Ally had to ease off the accelerator to avoid touching the rear bumper of the car ahead. Despite its size, it was surprisingly powerful and easy to handle. It was an upmarket sports model that Charlie had won in a competition. Even though he didn't drive it much, he loved it dearly. She wished Jim was in the car with her, driving. What would he do in this situation?

The answer came to her even as she flicked on her indicator and changed lanes. She sped up and then ducked quickly back into the left lane. Lights flashing in her rear-view mirror signalled she had cut it too close. Ally checked her mirror again. Now there were three cars between her and the white car. If it passed too, it would give away its intention. It stayed where it was, possibly thinking one more car wouldn't make a huge difference. A flashy red car was travelling in the right lane at speed and just before it reached her, Ally dived out again and accelerated. The car whined and bolted forward like a horse given free rein. Ally felt her back slam into the seat by the burst of speed. She flew down the wrong side of the road, passing two, three, four cars at once. A quick backwards glance confirmed the white car was following but they had lost precious seconds and were caught behind the red car.

Her fingertips were tingling and threatening to go numb and she forced herself to become calm and rational, like a Formula 1 driver. She let the small car have its head and it needed no more urging as it sped into the foothills. The white car was nowhere to be seen.

It was an exhilarating drive through the curves and rises. She had never broken the speed limit quite so thoroughly before. By the time she reached Withcott at the base of the mountain, she could afford to crawl through it at 60 and avoid the speed trap.

Soon she was starting to climb up the mountain to Toowoomba itself. She wove in and out of the traffic, leaving slower cars in her wake. Her car started labouring a little and she eased off the accelerator. The small car automatically changed down a gear, droned madly like an irate bee and began to pull itself up the incline.

The road had been carved into the mountain, which rose high on one side, while the other side disappeared, making way for an occasional dazzling glimpse of eucalypt forest far below and a view of the entire valley. Ally saw nothing but the road as she drove it too fast for comfort, weaving through the cars as if she was in a progressive dance, constantly changing partners, tantalisingly close for a second and then swinging away, eager for the next encounter.

Ally's ears began to hum, and she made herself yawn to equalise the pressure in her ear drums. The last turn was coming up. It curved and curved until she was afraid her speed would send her flying off the edge, until at last, the road evened out, still climbing, into the welcoming embrace of the city above.

It was a beautiful city at the best of times, with wide treed avenues and beautiful homes tucked into leafy gardens, but now in spring it was arguably at its best. Personally, Ally liked it in May when the autumn trees blazed in the mellow sunshine but this was spectacular. Bright flower beds dotted the vibrant green lawns on either side of the road. Peach trees, azaleas and magnolias graced many gardens along with masses of bulbs and blossoms that peeped through fences and occasionally replaced them entirely.

Was Nicholas here somewhere, hidden behind a wall of flowers? Their cheerful nodding heads gave nothing away. Ally glanced at her watch. She still had over an hour left. The white car had not appeared, but she knew it wouldn't be far behind her. She drove at a sedate pace, looking around her. Antique stores and galleries shared space with coffee shops and cafes to her left and an ancient park of dark green camphor laurels spread out to the right. This place was so close to Brisbane and yet so different. The atmosphere here was temperate rather than subtropical and the trees looked more European than Australian. Frosts would lie on the ground in winter and mysterious, cooling fog would swirl in the mornings.

Ally had seen the flower carnival once a few years ago but had been here in May quite a few times. She had come up to source handmade shawls to use in their romantic bedroom series but the sight of the maples had taken her breath away. Trees that had been indistinguishable from the other greenery would suddenly become flaming beacons in every shade from purple and red, orange and yellow. Thinking about Autumn made her homesick for the leafy maple that shaded her parents' front porch. The apple trees would be changing to a subtle bronze and the hazelnuts would be ripening. Her mother might be raking up fallen leaves right at this moment and dad would be on the porch, reading, and underlining the passages he thought were important, every inch the retired college professor. Ally was glad that the maples were invisible here today. The need to run to the safety of her parents' arms was so strong without any reminders. She thought of ringing them just to hear their voices but she couldn't. Not yet.

Where was the carnival? Even as she asked herself the question, Ally saw a glimpse of the Ferris wheel through the trees. It was at the far edge of the park, opening onto the start of the city centre. She flicked the indicator on and turned right, parking the car across the road. As she got out a cool breeze ruffled her hair and she was glad she had a warm jacket. She scanned for a break in traffic and dashed to the other side. As she made it to the footpath, she saw the white car on the main road driving straight through the intersection. She ducked behind a tree, but it had already driven past. The driver and passenger had been craning their necks as they drove. To see the Ferris wheel or to catch sight of her?

But why? She was an ordinary person for goodness' sake. Why were all these bizarre and violent things happening around her? Was Luke's brother completely insane? Luke was dead. What was the point of destroying his family? Nothing in the world could hurt Luke now so why kidnap her little boy? Ally realised she was mumbling to herself again. She was probably going crazy herself. A throbbing ache had started in her head. She rubbed her temple and breathed in deeply, trying to control the pain. The bruise under her fingers was spongy and sore.

She waited behind the tree for a while longer but the old white car didn't reappear. Relieved, Ally turned back to the carnival. It was like a flower themed sideshow alley of sorts, almost deserted at this time of day, except for a few carnies getting ready for the festivities that would start again at sunset. There was no point at getting any closer yet. It was still only a little after eleven. Ally looked around, trying to decide where to go. She wasn't hungry after that cheesecake and shopping was something other people did. Not someone caught in a personal nightmare. She wanted to be alone with her thoughts, she would go to her favourite place here. Making up her mind she walked back to her car.

The little car sprang away from the kerb, ready for action. Ally had to hold it back, or maybe it was her own anxiety she had to keep in check. The streets she drove up were so beautiful that they needed to be explored slowly, not driven through mindlessly. The one she was on now boasted an avenue of deep green Camphor Laurels which arched above the bitumen and met, intertwining their leafy branches. The air was filled with the clean scent of the leaves.

Houses with lacy verandas peeped out between the trees, each lovelier than the last, and everywhere there were flowers. Hanging baskets of sapphire Lobelias, beds of Cinerarias and fairy primroses, Wisterias climbing over pergolas with purple blossoms that hung down like bunches of ripe grapes.

The street led ever eastward and upward until it simply disappeared. The houses, the trees all gave way to a stunning expanse of sky and distance. If Ally had not been here before she would have been afraid of falling off the edge of a cliff. But at the last second, the road veered left and curved its way down again. Even so, she caught her breath at the view. After a careful U turn, she parked the car and climbed out. Webb Park, a series of grassy hills that led steeply down into the valley and merged with the eucalypt forest below. The air was crystal clear and as far as the eye could see, smaller hills and valleys stretched out like a tapestry of ever paler blues and greens. Ally sat down on the velvety grass, let her mind empty and simply looked out towards the horizon. It was so, so big she thought, relaxing. The taught muscles of her neck and shoulders loosened and she felt the knots in her jaw let go. The headache was gone. For a while, peace invaded every pore, every corner of her soul until it came to the locked dark place that vibrated with anxiety and fear. Then even the view couldn't help.

Would this be the end of the road? Would she find Nicholas today? Was he at the carnival already? Ally glanced at her watch. Only a half hour left. She became aware that she wasn't alone. Far below her, a young family played on the swings. The children's happy shouts brought a sudden stab of envious anger, swiftly followed by sadness. She couldn't bear to look at them. To her right an elderly man stood, with shoulders squared and a back as straight as a soldier's. A tricolour border collie burst from the scrub at the bottom edge of the park and tore up the hill towards him carrying a stick. She placed it triumphantly at his feet and sprang back, waiting alertly. The man lifted the stick and the dog darted sideways anticipating the direction of the next throw. Taking his time, the man swung the stick and Ally watched it fly through the air with the dog in hot pursuit. The man turned back and smiled at a woman sitting on a park bench in the shade of a pepperina tree. As if sensing his gaze, she looked up from the thick book she was reading, perched her glasses on top of her silvery curls and smiled back at him.

She was his wife. Ally knew it as surely as if she had been at their wedding half a century ago. They seemed connected despite the space between them. They matched so perfectly. Ally's eyes filled with tears. Would she even know such a deep and abiding love?

A sharp bark beside her made her jump. The dog had deposited the stick at her feet and panted, waiting impatiently for her move. The dog's rich brown eyes were deadly serious, this was no game. It barked again, a short, sharp commanding bark. Ally took the stick and stood up. As she drew her arm back, the elderly man came closer, shaking his head. He had a distinguished but friendly face that time had been kind to. His bushy white moustache tilted as he smiled at her. Ally immediately and without knowing why wanted to hug him and tell him all her problems. There are some people in the world who just look as if they can fix anything.

He took the stick gently from her and turned it around, handing her the thinner end.

"It will travel a greater distance if you hold it like so," he explained patiently in a faint European accent. It was fitting that she had met him here, on top of a mountain.

Ally nodded, then standing clear, she swung the stick and let it leave her hand. The dog had pre-empted her move and reached the spot where the stick would have landed first, twisting high in the air and catching it with a growl.

"She's very good," Ally nodded towards the dog.

"Zoya is a working dog, but I have no sheep for her to herd, so she has chosen the pursuit of the stick as her task. Everyone needs a special task to make their life complete."

"Someone has taken my task from me," Ally stammered. "My baby boy was taken."

"I see..." he looked at her with sadness and deep compassion. "I sensed a deep grief and disquiet in you as you sat, but this is even more terrible a thing than I could have imagined. I am so sorry for you. Is there anything I can do to help?"

"There's nothing. I am so alone."

"None of us is alone." Came the enigmatic reply. "There is an energy in the universe beyond imagination, and it is in ourselves also. Look into yourself and you will find the strength you need."

"But what if he's dead?" Ally blurted out her deepest fear.

"Death is only the logical progression of life. It is the next step in our development as part of eternity. It is not something one should fear, but if your little son has left this plane of existence, might you not feel it, deep within your soul? Do you feel that his light is no longer frozen into matter?"

Ally stared at the distant blue hills, willing herself to feel Nicholas. She wasn't psychic. No message came to her.

"I don't know, "she whispered, tears welling in her eyes.

He took her hand in his. His fingers were long and square with a surprising strength, that seemed to flow from him into her. Ally's tears were whipped away by the breeze and she saw him clearly. His eyes had faded to a soft light brown with flecks of green, his skin had tanned to an even brown and the hair under the brim of his felt hat was silver. He seemed as old as time itself and as eternal. So calm. This is what inner peace feels like, Ally thought, holding his hand tightly. She heard the dog bark again, wanting the stick thrown, but she couldn't move. She had to know what he was going to say next. Seconds passed.

"Then you must assume that he is alive, and you will find him."

"Do you think so?"

"I do not have to think. I know."

Ally read the certainty in his eyes and she became certain too. Nicholas was alive and she would find him. "You are so wise," she said. "Thank you."

"No thanks are needed. I wish you success in your endeavour." He let Ally's hand go and tossed the stick again. It flew even farther, into the scrub. Zoya didn't hesitate before plunging in after it. "We must be leaving," the man continued. "It was a pleasure meeting you."

"Likewise," Ally returned. The man joined his wife and together they walked up towards the road side by side. The dog caught up to them just as they disappeared over the rise. She hadn't even asked him his name.

The young family had also left, so she had the park all to herself. Ally sighed and looked at her watch. She had to go too. A sandstone monument in the shape of two Greek columns leaning into each other caught her eye as she started towards the car. On one side were inscribed the words.

ERECTED BY THE PEOPLE

GEORGE ESSEX EVANS 1863 – 1909

On the other, inlaid with black on marble was part of a poem. Ally lightly ran her fingers over the words and spoke them aloud so the breeze carried the sound beyond her reach.

Dark Purple Chased with Sudden Gloom and Glory,
Like Waves in Wild Unrest.
Low-wooded Billows and Steep Summits Hoary,
Ridge, Slope and Mountain Crest

Cease at her Feet with Faces Turned to Meet Her,
Enthroned, Apart, Serene,
Above her Vassal Hills whose Voices Greet Her
The Mountain Queen.
"Toowoomba"

"Wow!" Ally turned back to look at the valley. The "Waves in Wild Unrest" just seemed like ripples on a placid blue lake today. She said a silent goodbye to them as she left.

The carnival was still as quiet as it had been an hour ago. A high wire fence surrounded the stalls and Ally had a long walk before she found the entrance. Hot dog and ice cream stands greeted her, their fronts drawn and shuttered against the sunlight. Booths of wooden clown heads, their painted mouths wide open, sat silently staring. Ally felt their eyes on her as she walked past.

She had never been too fond of side show alleys but they had seemed harmless enough, not like this disquieting, half abandoned place. A huge bearded man stared at her unblinkingly as she walked past his booth of fluffy stuffed animals and rifles. She looked away nervously and tripped over a loose rock as she hurried to the Ferris wheel. The fairy tale giant chuckled behind her.

She walked past the haunted house and the smaller rides, before she reached the Ferris wheel, soaring majestically above the other attractions. The tall iron structure looked even higher when she stood in its midday shadow. A small ticket booth drew her attention. That is where she had to pick up her letter. The letter she had to read at the top of this thing.

As she drew nearer to the booth, she realized that it wasn't as empty as she first thought. A girl sat in the booth, waiting for her to come nearer. She was pretty but her gaze was bored and unfocussed. She showed no surprise at the unexpected customer.

"Hi," Ally greeted her, "I'm supposed to pick up a letter here."

With no change in expression the young woman pointed to the sign above her head. It said "$5.00 NO CONCESSIONS".

Ally fumbled in her purse and brought out her card to tap on the payment terminal. The girl reached down and brought out a large brown envelope. There were no markings on it, no clue of what was inside.

"Do you know who left this for me?" Ally wanted to know.

The girl shrugged, looking even more bored. The kidnapper was clever. He had chosen this place carefully. No one here would identify him. Fleetingly, she wondered what Jim would do in this situation. Would his smile charm an answer from the girl in the booth? Maybe scare it out, Ally had heard him swear. He wasn't here and there was no point in speculating. The girl kept looking at her vaguely and Ally thought she probably didn't know much anyway.

"Thanks anyway." Ally forced a smile as she turned and made her way over the trampled grass to the makeshift steps of the Ferris wheel. Each basket was designed to hold four, perhaps even six people. The metal seats were painted in bright colours that almost hid the bubbles of rust that were coming through. There was no one to help her up, so after a moment's hesitation she pulled herself onto the seat and hooked the safety chain up. The cold of the seats seeped through her jeans instantly and she wondered how long she would have to wait. Her watch said it was almost midday.

Suddenly the motor beside the wheel began to hum. Ally craned her neck but could see nothing. The Ferris wheel groaned, shuddered and jerked, then began to turn, lifting her basket off the ground. Seconds later it stopped abruptly so the next basket sat level with the stairs. Nobody climbed in. The cycle repeated for every basket as if an unseen hand was starting and stopping the wheel. Ally felt as if she was among the ghosts of people who once sat here, riding high above the earth. The wind blew harder up here and she shivered, whether from the cold or fear or both. She could see the road she had driven in on. Little cars moved this way and that along it like so many ants.

Straight ahead of her, she could see Charlie's car, parked on the side road. Further away, beyond the city and the houses surrounding it, the outline of the strange arrow shaped Bunya pines dotted the horizon. Before European settlement, indigenous Australians had gathered here each year when the giant cones of the Bunya trees would fall. The succulent nuts within would be gathered and cooked. It was a time of celebration.

Louise told her that Toowoomba was built in the crater of an extinct volcano. From her vantage point she could see most of the rim of it. It had coloured the soil a rich red which showed through the trampled grass of the park.

Finally, she was at the top. High noon. With trembling fingers, she started to open the envelope. Just then, the wheel started to spin. Ally cried out as she was thrown forward, just saving herself by grasping the nearest upright to hang on to, the letter gripped tightly in her palm, between her skin and the metal. The Ferris wheel spun faster and faster until the sky and the land merged into a grey blur. Her stomach heaved and tried to escape through her throat. She had not been on a ride since she was twelve years old and she had hated it then but now with it out of control, what she felt was beyond hate.

Ally squeezed her eyes shut and held on for her life. In a moment she was sure she would become airborne as the metal around her, clearly not designed for such speeds began to squeal. It was about to fly apart and collapse.

Then, just as she thought the crazy spinning would never end, the brakes came on and she was thrown clear off her seat and onto the bare metal floor. With a shuddering groan, the Ferris wheel stopped turning.

Ally opened one eye. She was still here. Her cheek was pressed against the floor and her knees and elbow hurt with new bruises. The basket continued to sway a little, releasing momentum. Cautiously, she opened the other eye and lifted her head. She was at the very top. Hers was the highest basket. Beyond the edge of the floor was nothing except deep blue sky. She was frozen to the floor, unable to move. The nausea eased gradually, but she stayed where she was.

Where was the letter? Ignoring the protests of her body, Ally raised herself onto her elbow. Miraculously, the letter was still clutched in her hand. Painfully, she dragged herself back onto the seat and peered intently at the ground far below her. Here and there a person was moving, no one taking the slightest bit of notice of the Ferris wheel.

Except one. It was hard to be sure, but it looked like a man who was sitting on one of the horses at the stationary merry-go-round. He was dressed in a dark hoodie that helped him melt into the shadows, but Ally could just make out the paleness of his face as he looked up at her. Certainly, he could see that she was in trouble. She waved at him, but he remained motionless. His utter lack of movement was menacing.

Was he the one who had left her the letter, who had sent her spinning out of control? There was no way she could reach him, or even be able to identify him. Ally looked down at the letter, dreading whatever was inside. When she glanced at the merry-go-round again, the man was gone. It must have been one of the kidnappers.

There was no point in putting it off. Taking a deep breath, Ally tore the letter open. The only thing inside was a photograph. She pulled it out slowly. It was a black and white picture of Nicholas obviously taken on the day he was abducted. He was sitting on the lap of a man in a dark suit and mask. Nicky's little round face was set in a stubborn scowl and Ally could make out the tell-tale signs of tears streaked across his cheeks. Answering tears sprang up in her eyes. Across the photograph slashed a streak of red crayon, narrowly missing Nicky's face. Her fingers clenched it until the envelope crushed into a ball of damp paper.

There was no other message in the envelope or on the photo, but Ally understood clearly. It was an explicit threat. Nicholas was still alive, but for how long? There was no demand. Nothing to explain what the kidnappers wanted.

Ally pressed the photograph to her cheek. Oh, her poor little baby, what were they doing to him to make him cry? Ally's mind began to whirr with terrifying images. She blocked the thoughts even as they came into her mind. She had to think of him as being well and happy and waiting for her, or she'd go mad. He was just crying because he missed her.

"I miss you too sweetheart," she told the tiny image of her son, "don't worry too much, Mummy is coming to get you just as soon as she finds you. And then we'll be together for the rest of our lives. I've got someone helping me find you. His name is Jim. You'd like him. He was Daddy's friend. He is big and strong and kind. We can all go to the park when you come home. We'll go on all the swings..."

She sat there on top of the Ferris wheel for a long time, removed from the rest of the world, feeling that Nicky was right beside her. That they were here together, at the carnival, riding high, laughing, talking. But finally, the cold wind of reality froze her completely and she started shivering.

She was alone. The wind from the south west blew straight from distant Antarctica. She pulled the jacket tighter around her. The wind whistled straight through it. How long would she have to wait before someone saw her? The carnival didn't ramp up till sunset. Below her more carnies were moving about, readying their stalls and rides. How could she get their attention? Yelling "HELP" was a bit melodramatic. After all, nothing was actually happening to her. She was just stranded here, freezing.

"Hey!" she called down half-heartedly, then more loudly. "Hey down there. Can anybody hear me? I'm up here!"

Nobody took the slightest bit of notice of her. She was too far up. If Jim were here, he would probably just swing his long legs over the edge of the basket and climb down. Did she dare try it? Ally tucked the photograph and envelope into the inner pocket of her jacket and stood up. The basket swayed slightly, like a flimsy boat on the water. Ally knelt on the seat and looked over the back of it through the polycarbonate sheeting that encompassed the basket. She looked for a way to climb out and hold on until she reached the maintenance ladder but it was almost impossible. Maybe if she was a stuntwoman, or an acrobat...the ground was so far below. Ally swallowed.

"I don't think so," she said to the wind. She was no acrobat. There had to be some other way. She could call the fire department to rescue her like the proverbial cat up a tree. No. She could call Jim and wait for him to come get her but she didn't want to face him in her time of failure. She could call Charlie, but she had his car. Ally leaned back onto the seat and looked up.

The long metal struts that made up the framework of the Ferris wheel were above her, the basket suspended from them with steel tubing. The maintenance ladder was within reaching distance from there.

Not giving herself time to think, Ally pulled herself up as high as she could and reached the strut above her seat with her fingertips. Tantalisingly close but a fraction too high. Wobbling a little and still looking up, she jumped, arms outstretched. This time her hands closed around the thick metal tube, but it was slippery with thick black grease. Her grip loosened and she felt herself falling back into the basket. She missed the seat and landed on her bottom on the floor. The basket swung violently, trying to expel her. She pulled out a tissue and wiped her hands on it. The grease wouldn't wipe off and the tissue disintegrated with the effort. All she needed now was a runny nose and if she stayed in this wind much longer, that would be exactly what she had. After a while she got up and sat back in the seat. There was nothing else she could do but wait. She closed her eyes and thought of Nicky.

When she opened them again, the sun was sinking lower in the sky, washing it with bright gold. She shielded her eyes against the afternoon rays to watch a silver car with the unmistakably beautiful lines of Jim's fastback pull up behind Charlie's compact. Could it be? No, that would be too much of a coincidence.

A broad shouldered man climbed out of the car. Despite the distance, she was sure it was Jim. He looked around, waiting for something. Or someone, a voice inside her head said. Sure enough, another car pulled up behind him. A white car. It could have been the white car. Two men got out and the three stood there for several minutes, before splitting up and walking in different directions. Jim walked across the road and entered the carnival. She would know that slow, seemingly casual walk of his anywhere. He looked dangerous and ready for anything as he glanced down at his phone from time to time.

Ally sank down in her seat and tried to make herself as small as possible. They were obviously looking for her. Jim was somehow connected to the two men who had followed her here. It was the only explanation that made sense. But why? Was he behind the kidnapping?

She felt unbelievably disappointed. Even though she barely knew him, she had trusted him, liked him. A lot. Too much obviously. The disappointment faded, giving way to twinges of fear. She was trapped up here, with nowhere to run. What would he do to her when he found her?

She craned forward to watch him as he drew nearer. He spoke with the bearded man who was lounging against his booth, then looked straight up at her. The giant must have known where she was the whole time. And the wretch had just left her here to freeze.

Ally cringed, huddling lower in the seat, trying, despite the utter futility of it, to hide from Jim. He had seen her of course. Ally saw him recognise her. He didn't react the way she had feared though. The sheer, honest relief on his face was visible even at that distance. Her suspicions evaporated like so much smoke in the wind. He was worried about her. He had been looking for her. He had found her. She felt herself flush from how quickly she had judged him.

Jim ran to the bottom of the Ferris wheel and expertly started the motor. Ally's basket jerked to attention and glided slowly downward. She was so sad and cold and tired, not to mention embarrassed that she couldn't even move to stand up. Her relief couldn't even break into a smile. Jim unhooked the chain and sat down beside her, hugging her tightly and holding her close.

"You little fool," he whispered into her hair, "you didn't even tell me where you were going. You just disappeared."

"I couldn't," Ally mumbled into his coat.

"Why on earth not? I thought we were in this together." Jim tilted her face up to look at him. She could plainly see how upset he was. "What are you doing here anyway, admiring the view?"

Ally said nothing. Seconds before, she had suspected him of being one of the kidnappers. Dishonesty wasn't something she was used to, especially in herself, but she couldn't bear to let him know of her suspicions. That would hurt him so much. Instead, she pulled out the crumpled envelope and the photograph and let him take them from her.

His face paled as he saw the photograph. He looked from the picture to Ally and back again. Something akin to despair showed in his eyes. Ally had spent the last few hours talking herself out of thinking the worst. Now a wave of fear left her nauseous and weak. He knew something. She could see it in his eyes.

"What is it?" she asked. "This proves Nicholas is alive, doesn't it?" She was trying to convince herself as much as him.

"Yes! Definitely! He's alive," he said with as much conviction as he could muster. "Was there a message? Any demands?"

Ally shook her head. She had started shivering again, and without a word he took his coat off and wrapped it around her shoulders. She snuggled into its soft folds. She closed her eyes and felt Jim's warmth enveloping her.

"We'll have to take this to the police lab. There may be some fingerprints left. They will analyse the photo too. It looks like someone printed it out on a home copier. That could lead somewhere."

Jim carefully tucked the envelope with its precious photo into the breast pocket of his shirt. He was in full control of his emotions now, completely professional, with no hint of the turmoil within. But Ally remembered how he looked when he first saw her stranded and alone on that Ferris wheel and stored the memory in her heart. He cared for her and she would never forget that. She would never doubt him again either. She was still looking at him with a silly, wistful smile when he said something else.

"I'm sorry, I didn't quite catch what you said."

"I was just asking how they contacted you."

"Someone called. Yesterday. A man I think, but the voice was disguised. He knew I was alone. He warned me not to tell anyone. I wanted to tell you, but I couldn't risk it. Please forgive me."

"Of course, I do. It's just lucky I had someone watching the house to make sure you were safe. They saw you leaving and followed."

"White, non-descript, dime a dozen?"

"Yes."

"I lost them," she said with grim satisfaction. "I thought they were the kidnappers."

"I hope you can forgive me for that, I can't forgive myself for scaring you like that. I should have let you know that they were there for your protection."

"Yes, you should have. I was terrified. I've been sure that someone has been following me for a long time now, months in fact. Ever since Luke..."

Jim winced inwardly, knowing it was his men who had not been careful enough. Had caused Ally so much fear, ever since Max Reed had ordered 24-hour surveillance. He should have realized that she was too intelligent not to have noticed them. He tried to lighten the mood, "they told me you could make it big on the race track. Especially in traffic. They've had advanced driver training but were impressed with your skills."

"I couldn't drive a nail into a wall at the moment, dreading the drive home."

"I'll get one of them to take your car home. You look done in."

"It's Charlie's car. He doesn't use it anymore because of his leg."

"Hmm," Jim replied. At the mention of Ally's neighbour, he felt the hairs on the back of his neck stand up. Something about him just didn't add up. He just couldn't put his finger on it. Probably just rampant paranoia. "Are you hungry? Let's get something to eat before we head back."

"Actually, I am a bit hungry. There's nothing like being stuck high above the ground for hours in the fresh air to heighten the appetite." Ally forced herself to be cheerful, even though all she could think about was that cruel photograph in Jim's pocket.

"I know just the place," Jim smiled. "You'll love it."

Ally nodded, but her thoughts had flown back to the photograph. The entire day had been a complete waste of time. Time she should have had with Nicholas. She was no closer to finding him. The only thing she did know was that whoever had him possessed a sick sense of humour, and a flair for manipulation. Was it the man on the merry-go-round? If she hadn't been trapped in that Ferris wheel, she would have confronted him, torn him from limb to limb to get to her little boy.

Jim knew from the look on her face that Ally had withdrawn from him again. He didn't intrude into her thoughts, merely took her by the arm and led her to his car. She didn't seem aware of the traffic around them or the open car door. Jim had to help her in as if she was a child herself. Even when his fingers accidentally brushed against hers as he was fastening her seat belt, she didn't react.

Was it just fatigue, or was she losing it? Drawing that streak of red across Nicholas' neck had been a calculated move on someone's part to unbalance her. None of his inquiries had produced so much as a single name. This someone was very clever and very dangerous.

Jim brushed some stray strands of the softest hair he had ever felt from Ally's forehead, then shut the door for her. Her skin was porcelain pale and the shadows under her eyes looked almost painful. She was dozing by the time he climbed in the other side.

He drove past more obvious, popular restaurants and headed to the northern outskirts of the city, where the highway rose again to the aptly named Highfields. Once a satellite village that had an almost rural paradise feel, not many fields remained, instead neat homes had sprung up on either side of the highway that doubled as the main street. At the edge of town, the thick trees gave way to a view of the entire valley and it was here that Jim turned into a circular driveway leading up to a gorgeous multi-gabled Victorian mansion with a deep porch set in a lush garden. The ornate façade was lovingly restored and brightly welcoming.

Ally woke with a start when the car pulled to a stop. She rubbed her eyes sleepily. She had been dreaming of holding Nicholas in her arms in fields of flowers. The short nap restored her hope. The man with the dog at Webb Park was right. She could feel Nicholas. She knew with certainty that he was alive and waiting for her to find him.

This place was so impressive yet tranquil, like a postcard complete with mountains in the background. Only a small sign near the front steps indicated that it was a restaurant.

Ally turned to Jim with a smile, "You were right, I do love it."

He smiled back, relieved that she had broken out of that trance. It was amazing what ten minutes of sleep could do for her. She looked so beautiful now that he wished he were an artist so he could capture this moment on canvas for all his lonely years ahead.

Jim opened the car door for Ally and she stepped onto the cobbled driveway. The scent of herbs from the garden carried on the early evening breeze. It was so quiet here. Only the sound of Currawongs calling to each other from their perches high up in the spruces edging the garden broke the sound of the breeze through the trees.

The superb glass door opened at the slightest touch. Inside, the sheen of highly polished hardwood floors sent a subtle glow up the flowing double staircase. The steady tick of a grandfather clock echoed across the foyer. Ally gasped as she followed the sound. It was the biggest and most wonderful clock she'd ever seen. Instead of the normal wooden box to house the pendulum, an entire forest scene had been carved out around it. Oak trees and firs formed the background, while deer, squirrels and rabbits inhabited the glade in front. The figure of a hawk had been etched into the silver of the pendulum. It seemed to fly from tree to tree as it swung, counting seconds.

As they watched, the clock began to whirr in readiness. The hour was approaching. The pendulum ticked once more and then the doors at the top of the clock opened and a parade of couples danced out of one side and disappeared into the other as the clock struck five. Louise would adore this!

Jim rang the brass bell on the small desk. The sound of footsteps preceded the bustling entrance of the owner. Her glowing rosy cheeks and sparkling blue eyes spoke of health and happiness. She wiped her hands on a snowy apron and welcomed them in. She looked as if she wanted to hug them tightly, and found restraining herself an effort. Ally found her open friendliness so appealing after the day she'd had.

"We're a little early for dinner," Jim began, "but would you be able to accommodate us?"

"Of course! We would be delighted to have you. Why don't you come and sit on the terrace while I fetch you a drink?"

"That would be lovely," Ally replied with a sigh.

And it proved more than lovely. The porch was magnificent, wide and deep. Pots of flowers and evergreens surrounded sumptuous cane outdoor settings. Silver lanterns glittered on the tables. But what made Ally gasp was the view. The terrace hung over a steep escarpment, the edge of the high fields as it were, and as far as the eye could see, blue treed hills stretched into the distance. The sun had set, so no glare distorted the clarity of the air and they could literally see forever. A band of pink sky slowly moved up from the horizon followed by an ever-widening band of indigo dusk.

Jim whistled in appreciation and Ally just said, "Wow!"

The meal didn't disappoint either. After a glass of orange Prosecco and home-made ciabatta, Ally chose a buttery chicken schnitzel with fresh apricot cream sauce and Jim settled on steak and chips. A warmth spread over her, whether from the long-awaited food, or the Prosecco or the company. All of the above she thought. They compared the places they'd been, the travel mishaps they'd encountered and the other meals they'd enjoyed. Ally began to lose herself in the clarity of his grey eyes in the lamplight, the flash of his even teeth as he laughed.

When other diners arrived the sounds of laughter and clinking lent the place an almost party like atmosphere around them while they sat in their own private sanctuary. After coffee, they leaned over the terrace railing. Warm white fairy lights twinkled in the trees echoing the flickering lights of settlements in the valley far below. To the right, the closer lights of Toowoomba blazed like thousands of fireflies spread out on a velvet blanket.

Ally leaned heavily on the railing. She was both tense and exhausted. "I'm sorry," she said at last. "I'm really not very good company."

Jim didn't reply for so long that she ventured a look at him. His face was serious in the dim light. "I don't know exactly what to say." He paused, thinking of the right words. "Of course, you can't forget what's happened and just have a good time. You're much too caring a mother for that. But even under these circumstances, there is no one's company I would prefer to yours." Jim caught himself. He had said too much. This was not the right time. What would she think of him? He pressed on, "If you like, we can make a date to come here with Nicholas when he comes home to show him that clock. It's something else, isn't it?"

Tears of gratitude filled Ally's eyes. He understood her so well. Her grief and guilt for being the one left standing while Luke died and now Nicky was gone. He didn't judge her. He was trying to give her hope for the future.

She put her hand in his and squeezed hard. "When we come back," she vowed, "I plan on buying that clock for him!"

"Even better, but do you realize how much racket those things make in the middle of the night?"

"I don't care." She laughed.

As if in tune with the lifting of her spirits, the sky to their right exploded with fireworks. Giant blossoms of sparks that lived and died in seconds. The cracks and booms followed well after the fireworks had disappeared in puffs of white smoke that followed the wind before also vanishing. It was magical and probably the best part of the Carnival. She would bring Nicholas here next year. It would be so exciting for him.

A scrape behind Ally made her jump out of her reverie. It was only the waitress. She was carrying a silver tray with two mugs of coffee and some chocolate.

"I don't know about you," Jim spoke softly behind her, "but I need a caffeine fix before heading back down the hill."

"Definitely," Ally answered. "Need the coffee and really, really need the chocolate. Thanks, this is lovely," she told the girl who smiled shyly as she set the tray down and left.

In any event, the coffee didn't help at all. The warmth of the car, her exhaustion and the hum of the

V8 combined to put her to sleep almost immediately, and she didn't wake up until they were on the freeway. Her head was pillowed on Jim's overcoat and she felt heavy and disoriented for a while.

Lying still, she listened to the quiet, measured sound of Jim's breathing. She was becoming used to having him around. In such a short time, (was it only two nights ago that they had met?) she had become quite dependent on him. When he left, he would leave another gaping hole in her life. And leave he would. He was just fulfilling the wishes of his friend to help her. She had lost Luke. Nicky was lost. She couldn't afford to get attached to this wonderful man and risk losing him too.

She made up her mind to keep her distance. To not get involved. But something told her that it may already be too late.

Jim couldn't help noticing how the soft sweep of Ally's dark hair fanned across her cheek as she slept. It was the sleep of exhaustion, deep and dreamless. He felt privileged that she trusted him enough to sleep while he was fighting traffic. After his early years at the orphanage, when furtive whispers and giggles signalled an imminent attack from the worst of the other boys, he had never been able to sleep unless he was completely alone, with the door locked. Even then, a part of him always remained alert, ready to defend himself. It would make having a long-term relationship a little tricky, he guessed.

Ally's eyelashes fluttered a little, then opened. "Where are we?" she asked sleepily.

"Almost home. It's funny, I haven't called anywhere home for a long time."

"That's so sad. You deserve to have a home of your own. Someone to come home to."

"Leads to misery in the long run," Jim joked.

Ally nodded, "I guess it does."

"I'm so sorry!" Jim groaned as he realized what his words had meant to her. "That was a stupid thing to say."

"It can be true. You don't have to be sorry. I'm pretty miserable, but I have the most wonderful memories. Being independent for so many years after Mum and Dad went home and I chose to stay behind, I was happy with my life of freedom. I really grew as a person and I could have stayed single easily and happily if Luke hadn't found me. But that was a lifetime ago. I don't regret my time with Luke, even if it did end so awfully. And it gave me Nicholas who is amazing."

Several minutes later, the car pulled into the driveway. It was the end of a very long day, with an even longer night ahead. Wide awake now, she doubted she would sleep at all tonight. The ache of missing Nicky had turned into a horrible, screaming pain that took up the entire universe.

MELBOURNE

Julian Roche left the old man's estate with a cool smile on his face and five hundred thousand dollars in his briefcase. Tall and whip thin, with long silver hair, ice blue eyes, chiselled features and dressed entirely in black, he was an impressive sight climbing into the sleek black European SUV parked at the kerb in the exclusive neighbourhood.

He never wanted for company. People thought he was an actor, or a photographer. Something artistic. Men and women alike were drawn to his cool looks and clipped British accent. The money and even the arrogance he treated them with was mesmerising. Once he was on a job however, he was single minded and intense, allowing no person or circumstance interfere with his objective.

Usually, he accepted a contract over the phone, carefully scrambled to prevent interception by the client or the authorities. His anonymity was important. He liked being a ghost.

This time had been different. The old man had found him and given him several alternatives. The only one not hazardous to his health had been a personal meeting. Julian was nothing if not adaptable to new ideas.

The meeting had been mercifully brief. The house was dark and oppressive. The old man himself was not someone he would choose to spend time with.

Despite the money and influence, he wore the mantle of death. An ordinary person may not have recognised it, but Julian Roche did, as he wore one himself. He had no conscience, no regrets, but he preferred not to look too closely at himself in the mirror, even one so distorted by age.

His purpose tomorrow was quite simple. The old man wanted two people dead. As usual there would be no witnesses and no evidence. Tomorrow he would be half a continent away in Central Queensland. The SUV, with a top speed of 342km/hr would get him there by morning. The fighter jet like dash included an electronic device to repel kangaroos and radar detectors to avoid speed traps the number plates were obscured. He could outrun a highway patrol car easily, but it was safer not to attract attention in the first place. The police presence was sparse and sporadic on the inland route he planned to take.

Driving through the night, he felt no fatigue. He was at one with his machine. He was a machine. He would not stop until his task had been completed.

Chapter Four

EIDSVOLD

Ally woke up to a blinding white morning. The river had disappeared into thick mist. Usually, she loved the mystery of fog, the shadowy forms in the distance, the muted sounds, the foghorns of the dredging barges as they passed each other on the river, the soft drip of water from the mango leaves in the back yard. Today it just intensified her feelings of being trapped and helpless. She remembered her mother saying, long ago, whenever it was wet, "At least we're all home safe."

"Oh Mum," Ally sighed. She had not rung her parents yet. Maybe tomorrow. Maybe a miracle would happen and she would not have to ring them at all until it was all over.

The landline rang. She rushed out of her room, but Jim had already answered it. He gestured for her to sit down. Taking a look at him, her heart leapt at

104

his expression. Two deep creases ran down his cheeks as he grinned at her. Cupping a hand over the mouthpiece, he said, "they may have been found."

Ally felt goosebumps on her arms as she hugged herself, not daring to believe that it was true. After he rang off, Jim took her cold hands in his and told her that a motel manager in Rockhampton had noticed two of his guests "sneaking" a bundle into their room which made him suspicious, so he kept an eye on them. One of the men had gone out and returned with grocery bags full of small tins and what looked like disposable nappies.

"I never feed Nicky tinned food," Ally protested indignantly, yet cheerfully.

"The description fits," Jim continued, "and the police have the place surrounded as we speak. I will organise a charter plane while you get dressed. You look way too good in that."

Looking down, Ally noticed that her pj's weren't very substantial. The fact that Jim was fully dressed in a suit made her feel practically naked. Flushing, she escaped to her bedroom to hurriedly dress in lightweight navy pants and white silk t-shirt, and added a jade sweater to ward off the early morning chill, although she wouldn't be needing it in Rockhampton.

She threw some of her clothes haphazardly into the overnight bag with Nicky's things which were still packed from yesterday. One thing was missing.

Hurrying to the kitchen, she pulled Teddy down from the window sill and tucked him gently into a corner of her bag. After a quick call to Charlie at his daughter's house to give him the good news, she was ready to go.

Only after they had left the fog of Brisbane far below, did she take a breath.

Waves of blistering heat assailed them as they stepped out onto the melting tarmac. The plane began to taxi away as they reached the terminal leaving a pall of fumes that didn't quite lift in the heavy air. Ally's t-shirt clung to her damp skin and she noticed how good Jim looked with his jacket off.

The door of a nearby car opened and Donna Marshal stepped out. She looked impossibly cool and efficient, even in uniform.

"What's the situation?" Jim asked her.

"The two suspects are still in the motel room. Our people are in position."

"What are you waiting for?" Ally blurted out as soon as they got into the unmarked police car.

"It's safer if the suspects make a move to come out," Donna said understanding Ally's impatience, "If we storm the place, Nicholas may get hurt."

Ally nodded silently and buckled up. Seemed obvious, but she just wanted to know he was away from those awful men.

Pulling up at a shopping centre carpark, Donna pointed to a low brick building across the road. "They're in unit 5."

Faded, blue and white striped awnings and dusty deckchairs gave the impression of a seedy motel trying to be a seaside resort and failing miserably. Nicky was in there. So close. Was he alright? Ally sat on her hands to stop herself fidgeting.

They waited for what seemed an eternity before Donna's radio came to life with a crackle of static. Police appeared from all directions converging on room five. Ally threw open the car door and followed. She dimly heard Jim calling her name as she raced to the motel. The police already had one dark suited man on the ground with his arm twisted up behind him while the other, taller one, was pushed against a wall being searched and cuffed.

A uniformed policeman emerged from the motel room carrying a child. Ally's heart gave one slow, painful thump, then started racing. She had expected to recognise him immediately but maybe it was Nicholas.

She called his name and the little one turned to the sound. Ally stopped dead in her tracks.

"It's not him," she whispered.

As if from a great distance she heard Jim say, "Impossible," before she crumpled to the ground. She felt the hot bitumen burning her cheek but couldn't move. Jim had to help her up and into one of the deck chairs in the shade. Then he was gone. Someone placed a cold drink in her hand and she sipped it automatically, not even knowing what it was. She saw Donna gesturing angrily to one of the local officers.

The nightmare wasn't over.

A moment later, Jim sat down beside her, wrapping his arm around her shoulders in a mute gesture of sympathy. She could feel the tenseness of his muscles through the thin material of her blouse. He bent his head close to hers.

"Don't react," he murmured quietly into her ear, "just get up and follow my lead. I've told Donna I'm taking you somewhere for a rest."

Ally threw him a puzzled glance but he lifted a warning eyebrow and she looked down again. Casually, he stood and gave her his hand. They slowly moved away unnoticed. As soon as they were out of sight, Jim picked up speed with Ally struggling to keep up in the stifling heat. He stopped for a few seconds to lift their bags out of Donna's car.

"Come on," he urged, "we don't have much time."

Ally detected suppressed excitement in his tone and an answering spark of hope flared in her. Clamping down on a dozen questions, she hurried in his wake for another block until he turned sharply into a car dealership. A young policeman man stood waiting next to a shiny black pickup, bristling with aftermarket attachments. The powerful engine throbbed under the bonnet and a shimmer of heat haze rose from it.

"She's my girl," the young man said proudly as he patted the truck. "Look after her, boss."

"Thanks, Rob, we will." Jim replied seriously. He released Ally's hand to open the door for her and she felt strangely bereft without his touch. She turned and climbed into the lifted vehicle. The air conditioner had filled the cabin with freezing air and Ally sighed deeply as she settled into the firm seat. It felt like a comfortable car inside, not the rugged off-road truck that it was.

Jim jumped up into the driver's seat and quickly pulled the seatbelt across his chest before adjusting the mirrors and taking off. Ally suspected he was speeding but said nothing. Within minutes, the WELCOME TO ROCKHAMPTON sign was disappearing in the rear-view mirror. Soon they were going so fast that the dotted line disappeared under the wide expanse of bonnet at a mesmerising rate. Unable to stay silent any longer, Ally asked where they were going.

"Eidsvold," Jim answered calmly.

"Where on earth is Eidsvold?"

"Not too far from here. About three hours."

"At this speed we should be in Brisbane by lunch!" Ally joked.

"This baby can really go, can't she?" Jim said happily, "she's been modified somewhat."

"Do you mind me asking why Eidsvold?"

"Has a great coffee house! Seriously though, they were warned."

"Who?"

"The kidnappers. I saw them at the airport, remember? Those poor fools at the motel were a distraction, probably paid to dress up in cheap suits and babysit some poor kid while the real ones took off with your son. Under the watchful eyes of thirty cops no less." The last bit worried Jim more than anything. How did they manage that trick?

"And you think they took Nicky to Eidsvold?"

"Let's just wait and see this time," Jim said. He wanted to say, I don't think I can watch you being so disappointed again, but he kept silent.

Ally leant her elbow on the window and gazed at the countryside flashing past. This was cattle country. Open and dry with small clumps of gum trees here and there amid pastures of brown grass. The small towns of Biloela and Monto were a blur and the smaller settlements in between disappeared in the blink of an eye. They only stopped once to fill up with diesel and use the service station restrooms.

During the drive Jim was quiet, and Ally followed his lead.

True to his word, he drove sedately into Eidsvold, just as the sun hit its high spot in the sky. It was a pretty little town with neat weatherboard houses trimmed with lush green gardens and picket fences. Huge fig trees arched over the quiet streets, providing dense shade. It seemed a quiet, sleepy town.

Actually, Ally thought as she kept looking around, the whole town was more than quiet. It was deserted. There wasn't a single car moving, no people, not even a dog.

Jim stopped at his famous coffee house, which was actually a tiny corner shop, to buy lunch while Ally waited in the pickup. She was becoming increasingly uneasy. Either everyone was having a siesta or they were in a ghost town. She shivered. Soon he returned with an armload of sandwiches, coffees and water. Ally was surprised that Jim had been served. She unwrapped a fluffy, delicious salad sandwich while Jim let the vehicle crawl along the main street.

"Uh oh," he said quietly, "Looks like we have a welcoming committee."

Ally looked up from her lunch to see about a dozen policemen spaced across the street. Squad cars and motorbikes formed a partial roadblock behind them.

The cop nearest the centre of the road motioned Jim to stop. Placing his half-eaten sandwich on the console, Jim pulled up centimetres from the man's shiny black boots. He rolled down his window and the policeman moved closer. He had an air of menace about him. Tall and broad with a hard, closed face, reflecting sunglasses hid his eyes. His right hand hovered near the revolver strapped to his hip.

"Please step out of the car sir," the policeman said. "We are searching all vehicles."

"As per the weapons act of 1994, I need to inform you that I am carrying a licenced, concealed firearm."

Ally started with shock. She had spent the last three days almost continuously with Jim and she had no idea that he had a gun. How foolish and naïve she was.

"Please step out of the car sir," the man asked again with frigid politeness taking a few steps backwards.

"I can see why everyone is indoors," Jim muttered under his breath. "Stay calm Ally, this will work itself out." He slowly climbed down from the pickup.

"You too ma'am." Ally turned breathlessly to find another cop at her elbow, next to the now open door. She scrambled down clumsily under his watchful eyes and felt herself flush with guilt even though she had no reason to. Jim on the other hand looked unperturbed as he was searched. The policeman stood back with a semi-automatic pistol he had pulled from Jim's shoulder holster and his wallet. From the latter he pulled a card and ordered one of his men to check it.

"You are in serious trouble sir," the cop ground out.

"And you need a lesson in manners, not to mention personal hygiene." Jim shot back. Ally felt the tension rise in the police around her and felt a bubble of fear in her throat. What if these men were connected with the kidnappers? They might die here in this silent little town and no one would ever know.

"Are you offering to teach me?" the cop was asking dangerously.

"Yeah," Jim drawled. Then he coughed, twice. Suddenly both men burst out laughing. The other officers looked on in confusion.

"Mike, you old dog, this is about the limit!"

"You liked it?" Mike laughed.

"Yeah. Now give me back the .45. Ally, I'd like you to meet Mike Wilson my foster brother. Mike, this is Ally Reed."

Mike pushed up his sunglasses to reveal warm brown eyes that twinkled with mischief. No wonder he hides them Ally thought as she said hello. He was too nice to be threatening.

"Sorry about the little joke, but this big buddy of mine brings out the worst in me." He sobered, "I'm hoping we'll be able to help you Mrs Reed."

"Please call me Ally."

"Ally then." He turned to Jim. "They're holed up in an old duplex in Campbell Street. We can walk. I've got the town sewn up tight. No one is going in or out."

Julian Roche wiped a minute smudge of mascara from his powdered and contoured cheek. He checked his teeth for lipstick. If one was to be a woman, it was worth doing it well. There was no substitute for glamour. Taking one last look at himself in the compact, he snapped it shut and slid it into his clutch where it shared space with his Glock. Someone was going to have one hell of a surprise.

Swinging his long shaved and fake tanned legs out of his sports car, he stood up, straightening the tight body con dress that hugged his thin hips. Were the stilettos too much? The driveway was uneven and bumpy. It took a few wobbles before he felt confident in his high heels. Felt good. Humming in a falsetto, he sashayed up to the front steps and rang the bell.

The short bald man who opened the door squinted at the sight that greeted him. Shaking his head in amused derision, he stood aside while his visitor swept past him in an expensive cloud of perfume.

"The old man said to expect a nurse, but he didn't say anything about a queen!" he guffawed at his own joke. "Hey Harry, come and look at what the cat dragged in."

Harry appeared a moment later, carrying an infant. Both were covered in sloppy food. He was nervous and twitchy. One look at the visitor and his pale face lost any colour it had.

Behind the heavy makeup, the glittering eyes of death looked at him. He had been waiting for his replacement with a mixture of anticipation and terror. One look at the man in front of him confirmed his worst fears. Instinctively, he brought the child in front of him, shielding himself. Being a coward was better than being dead. He knew his boss had plans for the boy and now he knew that the old man wanted him, Harry Jones, dead.

The visitor pursed his lips in a grotesque parody of a kiss and whispered, "the old man sends his love sweetie."

Seeing Harry's reaction, the bald man stopped laughing. Something was wrong. Harry was the brains of the operation, and if Harry was worried, so was he. He turned to run into the kitchen. The floor was the last thing he saw as something hit him from behind and exploded in his heart.

Harry began to shake as he saw his friend fall. The child poked him in the eye, but he didn't even notice. Fearfully, he looked back at the assassin. A small thick pistol had appeared in the manicured hand. It was fitted with a ceramic silencer. Harry had seen a gun like that in one of his firearm magazines. It was a Glock. A plastic and ceramic gun that was virtually undetectable.

Julian poked the body delicately with the shiny pointed toe of his shoe, then emptied another round into the back of its neck. Thoroughness was a feature of his work.

The assassin put the gun back into his purse and sighed dramatically. "Some people just aren't worth the effort."

Harry looked down at his friend and nodded. Was there any hope for him? "Is there anything I can get you? A cup of tea perhaps?" The assassin was British. They liked cups of tea, didn't they?

Julian Roche smiled coldly. It was like catching fish in a tidal pool. No sport at all. "No, not at present. Tell me about the child. What does it eat?"

"Oh anything, he's a good kid. His favourites are apple jelly and creamed chicken. He's no trouble, except at night, ah... just a little, you know, tummy trouble, I think. I could really help you with that." Harry could hear himself babbling, but he couldn't for the life of him stop.

"That will not be necessary," the assassin smiled. "Just put him down for a moment."

Harry shook his head, his eyes pleading, but he put the child down on the grimy sofa beside him and met his fate.

Julian put away his gun for the second time, hardly sparing a glance for the bodies on the floor. He bent down to pick up the child. It was softer and warmer than he could have imagined. It wriggled in his grasp. Roche looked down at the small boy he was holding. Nicholas looked back at him with happy, innocent trust and tangled his fingers in Julian's silver hair.

Julian blinked as he felt something tighten in his chest. Somewhere in the region where normal people have a heart. He felt his universe tilt and not right itself. What had just happened?

Ally walked between the two men. The crunch of their footsteps on the gravel was deafening in the sleepy afternoon. She was aware of the air leaving her lungs in gasps as she strove to keep up with them. Mike showed them to a small cottage opposite the duplex. It took all of Ally's willpower to stop herself staring at the building where Nicholas could be right now. They entered a dark, cool room which was frozen in time. The 1940's to be exact, with authentically aged rugs and yellowing army photographs. It was a little like being in a living museum. The owners were nowhere to be seen. Furniture had been pulled away from the windows and a plain clothed policeman sat there on a hard chair, peering through binoculars.

"Any changes?" Mike asked him.

"Yes sir. They have a visitor. A blonde woman in a black European SUV. A few minutes ago. I radioed it in but you were already on your way. She's only been in there a few minutes."

"Another out of towner," Mike commented dryly, "and one who managed to avoid the road blocks."

"I don't like it," Jim frowned.

Ally felt that something was wrong. The duplex was deathly quiet. Then she heard it. A muffled cry. It was enough.

"Tell me," she asked, feeling her skin crawling with dread, "does she have a baby seat in the back of her car?"

"Might have," the policeman conceded. "The back windows have a dark tint."

Ally didn't wait for him to finish. She was off and sprinting out of the house and across the road. At that moment, the sound of an engine growling shattered the silence and the black SUV came skidding towards her along the gravel driveway.

Ally saw huge sunglasses and bright red lipstick, then her attention was caught by the sight of Nicky strapped into a baby seat behind the driver. His eyes and mouth were wide open as if he was about to cry and his tiny hands seemed to be reaching out to her.

"Nicky!" she screamed as the car barrelled towards her, missing her by millimetres as it sped past. The engine roared as the car gathered speed and headed for the road block.

"Ally, are you alright?" Jim rushed to her side and pulled her against him. For a few seconds he thought she'd been hit by the car and he had felt like dying too. He had spent so much of his life deliberately alone and independent to avoid emotions like that, so the relief and intense joy that flooded him now left him stunned.

"It was Nicky!" she shouted to him, twisting out of his arms and running down the street. By the time Jim had caught up with her he had berated himself for being ten kinds of fool. He should have foreseen this. Mike's confidence had left him complacent. He was making far too many mistakes on this case because he was getting too personally involved. He was letting his feelings for Ally interfere with his judgement.

Any hopes that the roadblock had stopped the powerful SUV were dashed when they saw the disarray ahead of them. Several motorbikes and squad cars were already pulling out and flattened bushes on the footpath testified to the sports car's path.

With unspoken communication, Ally and Jim made for the pickup at a run. Mike caught up with them as they pulled out.

"Careful, Conrad. She is a nasty piece of work, "he warned, "She left two dead guys in that house. Looks professional. They didn't put up a fight."

"Damn," Jim breathed and his hand slid over to cover Ally's. This was the woman who was even now speeding off with baby Nicholas.

"We can't get any of our helicopters here in time," Mike continued, "but I know a farmer with a crop duster who can be up in twenty. She's heading south so we will intercept her on the highway asap.

"Thanks Mike, but we can't just sit here and wait."

"I understand, Conrad." Mike stepped away from the pickup and Jim gave him a nod as he backed up and spun the car around.

"Hang in there, Ally," he said as if sensing her fear. "At least we know he's alive and someone is going to a great deal of trouble to keep him that way. Now I think we were doing lunch when we were interrupted."

Ally looked at him, grateful that he was trying to inject some normality into this situation and to stop her slipping into hysteria. Although she had no appetite and the sandwich had become limp from the heat, she managed to eat the rest of it. It would do Nicky no good to have his mother faint with hunger, as well as fatigue. She leant her head back and closed her eyes, used to the frenetic pace Jim was setting. They had the road more or less to themselves.

She woke with a jerk and found the car stationary, idling with a deep rumble. Jim was standing across the road speaking with a highway patrolman whose car was parked facing them. With their perfect physical condition and close-cropped hair, they looked so similar that they could have been brothers.

"All he needs is a uniform," she thought groggily. They were both intent on a map opened on the bonnet of the patrol car. As if aware of her gaze, Jim looked straight at Ally. As their eyes met across the distance, Ally's breathing stilled and her heart missed several beats.

She had not felt like this since she had had a secret crush on the captain of the school swimming team. He had been tall and handsome and wildly popular and she had been a shy, clumsy bookworm. No one had ever known. She would have been mortified if even her best friend had found out. Once he had even talked to her. She had stammered some sort of lame response and escaped as fast as she could. He probably thought she was some kind of idiot.

Ally looked down at the hands folded in her lap, her cheeks aflame with remembered embarrassment. How could she continue to act normally around Jim now? Did grown up people still get crushes? She did not see Jim striding back until he appeared next to her, holding the folded map.

"She's disappeared," he announced as he climbed into the cab. Her embarrassment forgotten; Ally looked at him in dismay.

"It's a sports car, and it shouldn't be taken off road, but she's definitely not on the highway. I know it's old school but I can't see the big picture on Google Maps. This is where we are, just south of Tansey. This whole road has been covered both on the ground and in the air. So, she must be heading for Highway 1 cross country." Jim ran his fingers through his hair in frustration. "You won't find most of these tracks on a normal map because they are mainly private or forestry roads. They usually lead nowhere, but this one," he pointed to a faint dotted line, "will run all the way to the Pacific Highway because it joins this bypass road which is bitumen."

"That's such a gamble," Ally protested.

"I know," Jim conceded, "but we're out of options."

Ally nodded in agreement. They had already lost Nicky and the woman who had taken him under the watchful eyes of a dozen cops. They had nothing else to go on. Jim wasted no more time and typed the road name into the pickup's GPS. Within the half hour they were plunging headlong down a rough dirt track.

"Apparently the locals call this Seasick Road," Jim said cheerfully without taking his eyes off the track in front of him.

"I can see why," Ally returned through clenched teeth as the vehicle bounced in and out of the wheel ruts and big potholes. Boulders which had no business being on something called a road waited in ambush. And it got worse. The track began heaving like a rollercoaster ride with steep rises and deep gullies as the vegetation grew thicker and wilder. Ally gripped her seat and willed herself not to think of her precious Nicholas being shaken up like this. At least they were in a 4WD and it at least seemed to be enjoying itself. Maybe the movement had rocked Nicky off to sleep. When he had been tiny and restless, Luke would drive down bumpy suburban streets to put him to sleep. Ally tried to focus on the image of Nicholas sleeping. He always looked so angelic when he slept. Her phone was full of sleeping shots of her baby.

Jim spared a quick glance at Ally. She had that faraway look again. Sadness cloaked her features.

"Do you mind my asking what you were doing at the airport?" he asked the first question that came into his head.

Ally made a conscious effort to loosen her grip on the seat and looked at him behind the wheel before answering. At that moment, he reminded her a lot of her father – intelligent, good-looking and unfailingly considerate. She hadn't realized until now how much she missed her dad and her mum.

"I was taking Nicky to Canada to meet his grandparents. Family is so important."

Jim nodded even though he had no idea what that meant, never having had the love of a family. "What are they like?"

"Dad is wonderful. He is a retired language professor. When I was growing up, our house was always filled with books. He read Shakespeare to me at bedtime. Now he reads for pleasure and is writing his memoirs. People are always inviting him to be a guest speaker. I've seen him bring a room full of people to laugher and then tears with his stories. Mum is a complete contrast. She's immersed in life, not books. Unless you count racy romance novels. She looks fragile and delicate, but don't let that fool you," Ally chuckled. "She works as hard a two people. When I was a kid, she actually held down two jobs. I'm half her age and I can't keep up with her. She keeps their house in perfect order, as if she expects the people from House and Home to show up at a moment's notice. Instagram ready!"

"It must be hereditary," Jim remarked, as he swung the pickup around a particularly nasty pothole.

"Not likely, I am so messy compared to her."

"Your house is immaculate. But I meant your love of interior design."

"Oh, definitely, but you know, I have never been quite able to reproduce the feeling of 'home' like Mum did." Ally wondered if this road could get any worse. There did not seem to be any farmhouses or even letterboxes, only roughly hewn hardwood pickets strung with barbed wire delineating someone's property. They had certainly not passed any other vehicles since they left the highway. It felt as if they were heading nowhere, and away from any signs of life.

Jim dragged her thoughts back to their conversation. He was asking more questions about her family.

"No, no brothers or sisters. I was an only child, it was a really happy life, just the three of us. We came to Australia for a few years when Dad had a guest lecturer job at the University of Queensland and when they moved home, I decided to stay. It was the hardest decision of my life, not having them close by, but it made me a stronger person in the long run. I loved the relaxed way of life here, and the sunshine. But I was so lonely to start with."

Jim nodded, now loneliness was something he could relate to.

Ally continued, "Looking back, I guess I should have taken Nicky back home sooner but work was so busy, I couldn't leave Louise on her own. I just hope I didn't leave it too long and that soon mum and dad will meet my little boy."

"Don't even think that way Ally. We'll get him back. And when we do, you will make that flight. I may even volunteer my services as chief bodyguard, because now I want to meet them too."

Ally laughed, agreeing. Then she stopped. Something was bothering her. History repeating itself. Here she was, unburdening herself, telling her whole life story to a man she knew nothing about. A man who had not told her anything about himself. She had respected Luke's privacy and it had brought her nothing but grief. She would not make that mistake again. So, she just asked him.

"The story of my life is so corny it's just about embarrassing. I was found on the doorstep of a police station in a box, wrapped up in a sparkly pink t-shirt. Child Protection Services looked after me and I was brought up in a children's home in Sydney and a couple of foster homes. I must have been a bit of a wild child because no one ever adopted me."

Jim tried to keep it light but the bitterness and pain were close to the surface. He had no one.

"That's awful Jim, I'm so sorry."

"Don't be. It was actually fun sometimes. I learnt a lot from that place, like independence and how to make a great toasted sandwich."

But not love and family, Ally thought. Her heart cried for the little boy alone in the orphanage. She wanted to hug him and tell him that he did not have to be alone again, but the road was too rough, so she settled on just reaching over and touching him lightly on the back of his neck. The muscles were tight and corded. Unable to stop herself, she rubbed them until they relaxed under her hand.

"Thanks," Jim smiled, swallowing. The touch of her cool hand affected him more than he wanted to let on. He tried to concentrate on the road. "And the cop who found me visited a lot while I was growing up. He did want to adopt me, but the law was against him in those days. I used to call him Dad when we were alone. He brought me presents at Christmas and on the anniversary of his finding me. When I was older, he used to take me to work with him when he was doing paperwork. The police station was like a second home to me and those times were so special. He passed away when I was fourteen." His carefully neutral voice almost hid the sorrow of that time. "And when I was seventeen, I went to Uni and met my best friend, Luke. Good times."

Ally tried not to cry as she looked out the window. She did have to ask, didn't she? Now he had stirred up all those sad memories. She was glad though. He had not hidden his past from her, no matter how hard it was for him.

The track eventually flattened a little and started winding through a eucalypt forest. Tall grey gums blotted out the afternoon sun. the dimness was unnerving as it reminded them that time was passing far too quickly. When they neared the dividing range that ran beside the eastern seaboard, the track became a bitumen road, narrow, but a lot more comfortable. She breathed a sigh of relief and wondered why on earth people enjoyed four-wheel driving. The strong pickup effortlessly changed personalities into highway mode and surged forward.

Ally peered into the forest. They had just passed an isolated cabin buried in the woods, the first one they had seen for over an hour, when she thought she saw something shiny in the gully by the side of the road.

"Stop!" she called out. "Back up."

Jim slammed on the brakes and hit reverse. The huge wheels gripped the bitumen and rocketed them backwards.

"There," she pointed through the window. Jim leaned across her to look. She was acutely aware of his proximity, his even breathing, his strength. He turned to look at her, his grey eyes serious.

"I'll go down first," he said. "it'd be better if you waited in the car."

"Why? Oh no!" If it was the SUV lying there, Nicky might be in it, hurt. "Oh no." she repeated wrenching the door open.

"Ally," Jim held her fast with one hand, "it's better if I go have a look." He spoke slowly and gently. He hoped he wouldn't have to fight her on this. His even words reached through the maelstrom of fear and steadied her. She nodded, sagging against the upholstery. Jim gave her a quick nod of approval.

He eased himself over the embankment and made his way down to what was definitely a black car, partially obscured by vegetation. Ally squeezed her hands together in mute prayer as he bent to look inside. He straightened and waved to her. She followed, slipping and sliding down the soft, leaf strewn ground in her haste.

The car was abandoned and it was obvious even to Ally's inexperienced eye that the branches covering it had been placed there deliberately.

"There's no one inside," Jim told her with relief, "and the bonnet is still warm which means they haven't been gone long."

"I think that woman is finding out how inconvenient and time consuming it is to travel with a baby," Ally said with relief and grim amusement. It was an inconvenience she would give anything to have again.

"We now have one small problem," Jim ran his fingers through his hair in the gesture Ally now knew signalled his frustration. He would not make a good poker player. Even as he spoke, she remembered that they had no idea what sort of car the woman who had Nicky was driving now. Their only lead was sitting in a gully covered in twigs. They had reached the end of the road. Her baby was lost forever.

Ally felt her strength drain away, she was so tired and she just wanted to lie down among the fallen gum leaves and sleep forever. Jim looked down and knew that she was giving up. His heart tore at the sight of her despair.

"We'll find him," he said with all the certainty he could muster. She wasn't listening. He grasped her slumped shoulders and bent down to kiss her. He meant it to be a quick, reassuring brotherly peck, but as soon as he touched her lips, the world he had known shattered and the pieces washed away in tumultuous waves of need. Her lips were soft and sweet as they met and matched his kiss. Her body moulded to his perfectly. Her softness completed his strength. This is my woman, a voice inside his head said.

"How about you two get a room?" croaked a nasal voice behind him. He felt Ally recoil in shock, her eyes wide. Spinning around, Jim found himself facing twin barrels of a shotgun. Behind it crouched a wizened old man with a nasty crooked grin. Long grey hair under a moth-eaten hat, several teeth missing, gave the man the look of a story book witch. If a black cat had appeared beside him, the picture would be complete.

"You can forget celebratin'," he warned, brandishing his weapon. "I found it. It's on my land and you're trespassin'."

"You mean the car," Jim guessed.

"Too right, sonny," the man replied. "You know that's what I'm talkin' about."

"She's all yours," Jim assured him, trying to keep his voice casual. "We were just checking that no one was hurt. You didn't happen to see what happened to the driver did you?"

"I might have..." the old timer said cagily. He might be old but he wasn't stupid. These people were very interested in the people who had invaded his domain today without so much as a by your leave. This might turn out to be an even more profitable day. He shuffled closer, lowering the shotgun a little. "What's it worth to you?"

Jim reached into his back pocket and produced his wallet. Pulling out a fifty, he offered it to the old man. They shotgun lowered all the way and the man snatched the note in a wrinkled brown paw. He checked it carefully, before tucking it into the pocket of his grimy denim overalls. It was one thing to have a fancy new car, it was probably stolen anyway, but it was another to have cash in his pocket. He suddenly felt much more mellow towards these folks.

"Call me Mac, everyone does, not that I see anybody out here in the sticks. This is about the busiest this road's been since the bushfires. We had the rural firies, the army reserve, truckloads of them. Geeze, they worked hard, but the wind beat 'em. Caught my old shack and it went up like a torch. Had to rebuild, but that didn't take long. It ain't a palace or anything." It seemed to Ally that Mac hadn't talked to anyone in a very long time. The words rushed out of him like a dam bursting. The old timer wheezed in what was probably his idea of a laugh.

"Mac," Jim prompted, "the car?"

"Yeah. He had it waitin' most of the day. Someone left it this morning. It sure was a fancy one."

"You wouldn't happen to know what type of car it was?" Jim asked, not really expecting an answer. Mac didn't look like an automobile aficionado. Mac put out a hand expectantly. Jim shrugged and gave him another fifty.

"Another German tank, mate. Real fancy. I snuck in close for a peek but I didn't let that young man spot me. He looked kinda sneaky. And he had a pistol. Do you want the licence number?"

Ally gasped. Never had she expected such luck. Nicholas, she thought, mummy is coming to get you soon. Hang in there, little man. "Was she alone?" she interrupted Mac.

"Who?"

"The driver of this car."

Mac cackled wheezily. "That was no woman. Had long blond hair and a frock like a sheila, but it was a bloke all right. Unless it was the bearded lady." He cackled again at his own joke. "You two might be city folks and educated too, but you sure don't know much about the difference between a heifer and a bullock."

Ally and Jim exchanged glances. Could it be possible?

"Had a kid with'im too. Real cute little thing he was. About yo big." He bent down and put his gnarled hand palm down against his knee indicating Nicholas' height.

"Was the baby all right?" Ally moved closer to Mac.

"Seemed to be," Mac peered at her. "You're his mum, aren't you? Looks like you except for the hair. They've only just left you know. If you get a move on, you'll catch em pretty soon."

Jim shook the old timer's hand. "Thanks Mac, you've been more help than you could ever imagine."

"Enjoyed the company." Mac grinned showing the remaining yellowing teeth. "If you ever find yourself in this neck of the woods, come in for a cuppa. Bring some scotch, we'll have it Irish and have a yarn."

"We will," Jim promised as they made their way to the car and began the chase again. He was conscious that their task would be simplified by calling Mike, but he wouldn't risk police involvement this time. The fewer people who knew about this, the better. For all he knew the kidnapper had a police scanner, or worse, someone on the force was involved. How had he been able to dodge the roadblock at Eidsvold?

The pickup sped south towards Brisbane on Highway 1 for hours and passed many cars, but none of them was a black German SUV. Jim didn't really expect them to catch a European sports SUV with a huge 4WD, even if it was modified and ignoring the speed limits. But he was counting on his counterpart needing to stop at some stage to look after the toddler. He could feel Ally's tenseness in the seat beside him. Her fingers gripped the console at her side until the knuckles whitened but she didn't say anything as he wove in and out of traffic.

He picked up her hand and held it gently while he drove. Her fingers were cold and tense. He rubbed his thumb slowly over the back of her hand, feeling the tendons under the smooth skin. She had beautiful hands with slim but strong fingers and short unpolished nails. Ally sighed, closed her eyes and let herself enjoy the comfort of his touch. She was wound up so tightly, trying to catch a glimpse of a car that just wasn't there and he must have felt that. He was so thoughtful. She felt herself drifting off.

He held her hand until his went numb before letting go reluctantly. She made a tiny sound of protest in her sleep.

As the sun's rays lowered and the shadows lengthened, they passed through Maryborough and Gympie. A perfect evening deepened into night when they entered the sprawling outskirts of Noosa. Even though they couldn't see the ocean yet, its indefinable presence was carried on the sea breeze. Ally rolled down her window and breathed in deeply. Years ago, she spent her family holidays here. Even though the years of progress had transformed the once sleepy little town into a gorgeous tourist hub, the memories were strong. The warm, sunny days and balmy nights had woven a peaceful magic then and its echo soothed her tattered nerves now.

Despite the late hour, the streets were packed with slow moving cars and the footpaths teemed with strolling tourists. The black pickup stopped at one of the roundabouts and waited for the line of traffic to precede them. Ally twisted in her seat to look at Jim. He was alert, watchful, scanning the streets, looking as if he had been the one sleeping the afternoon away. As if aware of her scrutiny, he turned his head in silence. His grey eyes sparkled reflecting the blue lights of the dash. He smiled, a long, slow, hazy smile. Time ceased.

A horn sounded impatiently behind them, breaking the spell. He tore his gaze away from her and entered the roundabout.

"Nicky's here." As she said it, Ally knew it was the truth. The kidnapper would not be able to keep driving through the night with her little boy. Nicky would need changing and feeding and play time. "That man would have to have nerves of steel to put up with Nicky hungry and crying all this way. But where would he be?"

"That SUV is pretty distinctive, even for Noosa. And expensive. He'd want to tuck it in somewhere cosy and safe too." Jim frowned. "Assuming he doesn't live here, it will have to be one of the resort hotels on the Esplanade. Preferably one with underground parking. We should start at the northern end of Hastings Street and work our way down."

Before long they were walking along the most famous street on the Sunshine Coast. Open air restaurants vied for space with exclusive boutiques and art galleries. Beautiful, carefree people strolled along the footpaths and beyond the shops the shining resort hotels rose. Ally felt wretched and tired, "I hope they have a bathroom close," she murmured.

As Jim made enquiries at the first hotel lobby, Ally found a resplendent marble bathroom and freshened up. After splashing cold water on her face and brushing her hair, she felt a little better and ready to join the search. By the fourth hotel, she was exhausted again. Jim was at the counter, making enquiries and Ally stood beside him, not really concentrating. She looked around at the impressive foyer. Gleaming white floor tiles reflected palms and glorious colourful oceanic abstracts. Groups of comfortable occasional chairs circled coffee tables stacked with glossy magazines and flickering candles. She made her way to one of the chairs and sank into it. Her body was so weary, but her brain churned, knowing that she might be in the same building as Nicky.

The softness beneath her suddenly became nauseating. She stood and at that moment, the bronze mirrored lift doors opened.

A man dressed entirely in black with silver blonde hair stepped out. He carried a small child on his hip. Ally froze. She would know the back of Nicky's head anywhere. Just then, the child turned his head and Ally had to choke back a cry of joy. It was Nicky! She looked around wildly, trying to find Jim. He was a few steps behind her. Her tension communicated to him and he frowned. Wordlessly she pointed towards the blond man.

Jim took the final step towards her and whispered in her ear. "Is that Nicholas?"

She nodded, happiness bubbling its way through her body.

"I don't think we can wait for the police, Ally. He could disappear into the crowd in a second. If you ask me, it's payback time. How about we pull the same dirty trick they played on you. His hair is so pretty." He grinned wickedly.

Ally smiled back, liking the way his mind worked. "You pull, I'll snatch." They gained on the man quickly.

Working as one they reached him. Ally kept walking as Jim reached out with both hands and dragged the man's long hair down, pulling him off balance.

"Now!"

Ally spun around and grasped Nicholas, holding him as tightly as she dared. It brought her inches from the kidnapper's face. He was wearing expensive cologne, sweet and feminine. She looked into his pale blue eyes and felt a chill. Even fringed with thick blonde lashes, they stunned with the ferocity of the cruelty that lurked in their depths. Rage and pain contorted his features and drew his mouth into a snarl. Nicky whimpered as the man's grip tightened. Ally was so scared that he would hurt her son, that her grip loosened. Jim reacted quickly and converted to a relentless choke hold. Finally, the blonde man released Nicky and Ally stepped back, still holding her precious little boy. She sobbed with relief. He was alright. Her baby was safe and in her arms. She smoothed his hair back off his brow and kissed him, looking over the top of his head at Jim with gratitude.

He looked back at her, and Julian needed no other distraction to jerk out of Jim's hold and aim a kick into his stomach. Jim sidestepped, grasping the oncoming foot and twisting it with enough force to send the kidnapper down to the tiles. Roche fell and rolled away, coming to his feet in one fluid movement. Jim faced his adversary impassively, prepared for the next charge.

Ally was vaguely aware of gathering guests, but her eyes were riveted on the battle before her. Nicholas burrowed deeper into her embrace.

Roche lashed out with a vicious blow aimed at Jim's head. Jim deflected the move with a seemingly simple and delicate wrist movement, then, wrapping his fingers around his opponent's hand, he pulled him sideways and sent him reeling with an uppercut to the chin. There was a sound of teeth slamming together and a grunt of pain.

Picking himself off the floor again, Julian glared angrily at Jim. He was clearly unused to being on the receiving end in any confrontation. His anger tightened his muscles and narrowed his field of vision. He saw only the calm face of the man who was humiliating him. He spat a virulent curse at Jim in a guttural voice at odds with his carefully cultivated British accent.

Jim smiled slightly at the other man's language. He appreciated a good curse now and then. The smile provoked Roche even more and he lunged wildly. Jim waited for a split second, judging where the punch would land, then pivoted on his left leg and met the attack with a right kick that drove the wind out of

Julian's lungs and left him doubled up and gasping on the cold white floor.

Without taking his eyes from the blonde man, Jim walked over to Ally and Nicky and wrapped a protective arm around them. A few seconds later, the hotel security guard arrived and stood over the prone kidnapper until the police arrived. Ally released a long breath as she saw the ever- menacing pale skinned man being led away in handcuffs. As he reached the entrance he turned and looked at them. No, Ally thought, chilled to the bone, he only looked at Nicholas. His mouth moved, as he said something that didn't carry through the background noise, then was taken out of the door. It was finally over. She held Nicky close and leaned down to nuzzle his golden head. Nicky's chubby arms wrapped around her neck.

Jim looked down at mother and child with deep satisfaction and another emotion with which he was very unfamiliar. Ally looked up at him, green eyes glistening with happy tears and thanked him. He grinned and shrugged. The relief left them spent, so they made their way back to the seats. Nicholas wriggled in her arms, he had had enough hugging and was now impatient to play. Resisting the urge to restrain him, she let her arms relax and the tiny boy slid off the chair and stood next to it, tugging at the fabric. He looked none the worse for his ordeal. Ally gazed at him lovingly, she would never tire of watching him.

The next half hour was spent answering questions as the local police were brought up to speed. Jim also rang Donna and Mike to update them. The hotel treated them to a beautiful hot meal and even a box of toys for Nicky to play with. Euphoria had magically removed her fatigue and Nicholas played at her feet looking fresh enough to having had slept all day. Which, Ally guessed, he had done.

A television crew from Brisbane arrived a short time later. She recognised the reporter and her cameraman. They both looked genuinely glad at the happy ending to the story and their exclusive first interview. Ally didn't much care, she beamed into the camera and thanked the media and the entire country for its help and support. Everyone then focused on a happily unaware Nicholas pushing a toy train across the floor.

Sometime after the interview, Donna, who had arrived in a helicopter, sat down next to Ally. "So, this is the little cutie we've all been looking for? He's gorgeous Ally. Now that this is all over, I can tell you that I was extremely worried. The fact that there was no ransom demand, and those two men who were killed in Eidsvold."

Ally shivered. "I wonder why he did what he did."

"We'll know more when we've questioned him. Did he say anything to you?"

"We didn't really give him a chance, I guess, sorry."

"That's fine, great outcome all around. We will be transporting him back to Brisbane tonight. Will you be going home soon?"

"I don't think I could even get up out of this extremely comfy chair." Ally sighed happily. It had been such a long day.

Jim appeared beside them. He nodded a greeting to Donna, then turned back to Ally. "I've arranged rooms for us here, so we don't have to do any more driving today."

Ally sighed with relief. She reached up and put her hand at his. "I can see myself thanking you a lot for today!" she laughed.

CHAPTER FIVE

Melbourne

The old man sat at his desk, rigid with anger and hatred. A dark wood panel had been moved aside revealing a wide screen television. The monitor was filled with the radiantly happy image of Alexandria Reed, almost unrecognisable from the distraught woman of a few days ago despite the violet shadows under her eyes and the fading bruise on her cheek. She was thanking everyone for their help. The camera focused to show a young child playing beside her on the floor of what was obviously a hotel lobby. The small boy was oblivious to the attention. Ally whispered something to him and he looked up momentarily.

The old man practically choked on his own bile. The family resemblance was startling. Golden brown hair and eyes so like all the men in his family. He had wanted only the child. The woman meant nothing to him, however, now that she had interfered with his plans, she would also have to pay.

He would trust no one this time.

Alexandria and Nicholas Reed would die soon and he would watch the last of their lives drain away. Just as he watched his son die. His son's death must be avenged. The score must be settled.

Noosa

After the excitement had died down, Jim took Ally and Nicky up to their rooms. Mindful of the publicity, the manager had given him the keys to the penthouse suite. It was an enormous four-bedroom apartment with the kind of restrained luxury Ally had only seen in the movies. The walls were painted the softest blue grey with silver and white furnishings. Exuberant tropical plants provided colour. It was perfect, she thought.

Before they had even relaxed the doorbell rang and bellboys entered with armloads of boxes. A silver tray of tiny sandwiches and desserts was brought in and placed on the mercury-glass coffee table. Ally sighed, it was like a dream, just when she thought the day could not possibly get any better, chocolate appeared.

Finally, everyone left and peace enveloped the apartment. Ally sat on the floor beside Nicky who was attacking the presents with delighted laughter which was contagious.

The sound of Ally's laugh entranced Jim because it was so rare. Most of the sadness had left her eyes, but some wistfulness lurked close to the surface. He realised that he had fallen under her spell gradually, during his surveillance. He had watched helplessly as she struggled with the mower, his arms ached to help her carry the groceries up the steep back steps. His heart echoed her tears when she was alone and thought no one was watching. Being close to her these past days had intensified his emotions. When they kissed in the forest, his control had almost slipped. If that old man hadn't interrupted them, he might have blurted out that he loved her. Stunned by this revelation, Jim slumped in his chair, afraid she would turn and see the truth in his gaze.

The spectre of Nicky's kidnapping had been like a wall of honour for Jim. It was due to his carelessness that those two idiots had been able to attack Ally at the airport and take her son. It had been up to him to correct his mistake. Somewhere along the line it had become more than a matter of pride, but he kept that wall up. Now it was crumpling around him. The relief he felt knowing that Nicky was safe, washed over him, even as the reason he had to keep Ally at arm's length evaporated. He felt protective of them both now. Nicky was a handsome little boy, with hazel eyes and sandy hair and a tiny face incredibly like Ally's. Jim knew from his surveillance that he wasn't always so quiet but usually a handful, but he thought that the pleasure of watching him grow up would be more than worth it. For the first time in his life, he envisioned a future in which he would not be alone.

Jim vowed to tell Ally the truth and if she could forgive him for his deception, then maybe they could be together. Perhaps even another child. He daydreamed wistfully of a little girl playing with Nicholas and giggling happily as the little boy was doing now, delighting in the wrapping paper strewn over the floor even more than the presents. Along with toys there were clothes for both mother and son, disposable nappies, shoes. Ally realised these gifts were things she needed, right now and knew without doubt they were from Jim. She looked up at him from the floor and surprised a look of silly happiness in his grey eyes.

"Thank you so much," she said echoing his joy. She wanted to say more, but now was not the time. Not yet. Now she wanted to be with her baby, to reassure herself that he was safe. Soon after his bath and some crazy happy running around he fell asleep in her arms. She tucked him into her bed, ignoring the dainty white cot in the corner of the room. Quietly, she took Teddy out of her overnight bag and placed it beside Nicky. When he woke up, he would see his little friend.

Dimming the lights, she lay beside him and watched him sleep. He was so perfect. Her eyelids felt so heavy... Ally drifted off into a deep dreamless slumber.

When Jim checked on them, they were both sleeping soundly with the lights still on. He dimmed them and quietly closed the door. It wasn't until he was back in his own room at the other side of the suite that he got out his phone.

"Max."

"Good work, Conrad. I've just seen it on the news. There will be a bonus in this for you if you stick to them like glue until they get home."

"I was planning to anyway, Max." Jim didn't know what his client's reaction would be if he knew just how close he and Ally had become over the last few days. Even though Max and Luke hadn't been close for a long time, he doubted that the older man would approve of his involvement with his brother's widow.

As if sensing something, Max broke into his thoughts. "She's really something, isn't she, my sister-in-law?"

"Yes, she certainly is." Jim strove to keep his voice neutral. "This ordeal has been hard on her though. She and Nicholas need a rest. We'll be staying at the coast for a few days."

"Just make sure they're safe. I've made enquiries about the man they have in custody. Name's Julian Roche. German father, British mother, educated at Cambridge in political science. He's very expensive, a hitman, very good according to my source. I didn't want to interfere in her life but this is too serious for me to stand back. They killed my brother without warning, now they've attempted to take my nephew without a ransom demand. I don't like not knowing who my enemy is."

Jim didn't ask how Max had gotten the information so quickly, but he could imagine the other man's frustration. All his power, his influence, useless with an invisible enemy. An enemy that struck with ruthless precision, attacking the people Max Reed loved above all else.

"A favour, Max," Jim asked.

"Name it."

"I want to tell her myself."

"Fair enough, but don't take too long to do it. Because I plan to reconnect with my family very soon. Take care of them."

The phone went dead. Thoughtfully Jim cradled it in his palm. The hotel suite was so quiet, he could almost imagine that he was the only one here. After a lifetime of savouring his independence, a week in the company of Alexandria Reed had changed him fundamentally. He couldn't stand his loneliness any more.

When he told her the truth, she would probably never want to see him again. Every part of him rebelled against the thought. If he could only put it off for a while longer, maybe she would fall in love with him as much as he loved her. Could she love him enough to forgive him for spying on her, lying to her, betraying her trust?

Stop kidding yourself Conrad, he chided himself. A few extra days wouldn't make the slightest bit of difference. What he had done to her was beyond forgiveness. He knew how Ally felt about honesty and trust.

But could he give up the last few days of happiness he might ever know? Each second was precious when he spent it with Ally. Telling her the truth would be the hardest thing he would ever do, but he would not delay the inevitable. He would tell her as soon as she woke up.

Ally opened her eyes to find a little head lying across her stomach. It wasn't a dream. Nicky was really here. "Thank you, God," she whispered fervently. She stroked his soft gold hair gently so as not to wake him. Long lashes swept his round cheeks as he slept, making little snoring noises. It was the sweetest sound she had ever heard.

The bedside lamp cast a soft pink glow over the room. The hotel clock showed 10.00pm. She had slept for only two hours, but it had felt much longer. After lying in the luxurious bed for a few more minutes, Ally knew she couldn't get back to sleep for a long time. Gently, she cradled Nicky and eased out from under him to sit up. Her clothes were crumpled and she felt a bit sticky from the longest day of her life. Was it only this morning that she had woken up in her own room in Brisbane to the fog and the fear of never seeing Nicky again?

Stealing into the bathroom and stripping off her dusty clothes, Ally sighed with relief as a blast of warm water washed over her from the rain shower. She could get used to this luxury, she thought, wrapping a thick bath sheet around her and sampling the classy moisturiser provided by the hotel.

Jim stood on the balcony, watching distant beacons flashing on the horizon. They guided ships on their way to safe harbour, to port. He felt a little like those ships, guided inexorably towards Ally. Even before he had seen her, he had been drawn to her.

Max Reed had been contracting him to investigate some possible industrial espionage, when he called him in one morning and told him he had a more important case. Something he could trust only to Jim. He had been more than a little intrigued. What could be so important? Luke's widow was in some sort of trouble. Max did not specify what kind of trouble, an omission that probably facilitated the kidnapping. Jim was to fly to Brisbane and watch over her, from a distance. Max was adamant that Jim not reveal himself to the woman who had been married to his old friend, but to protect her from some unknown and unseen danger. He was not sure at the time whether Max himself knew where the danger would come from.

He had researched her website and had been impressed by her designs and captivated by her image. A little taller than average, with soft auburn hair that skimmed her shoulders and sparkling eyes in a shade of emerald green that he would not have believed possible, with long veiled lashes. Her nose was straight and refined and her cheekbones were high with smooth creamy skin. Her lips...here Jim had to stop himself. To remind himself that he was a professional, entrusted with her care, not someone to take advantage of her vulnerability, to remember how she captivated him from afar.

Despite her serene beauty, there was a constant shadow over her. Her eyes were always filled with sadness. She smiled rarely, unless she was with Nicky. Sometimes through his binoculars, he thought he could detect fear in her actions, but his background check had revealed nothing that would put her in danger. She worked as an interior designer, hardly a profession that produced enemies and she had not so much as a parking ticket to her name. But she had been married to Luke who had been killed in a car accident, which in retrospect may have been less of an accident and more of a deliberate crash.

Even now, the entire situation seemed bizarre and inexplicable. There was no discernible motive for Luke's death and Nicky's kidnapping. It was a nagging and unpleasant situation and the arrest of the blonde man didn't tie up the loose ends. Someone had hired him, but why?

The answer, as Max Reed had implied, must lie in Max's own life, not Ally's. And Max was not about to confide in Jim. He made a mental note to call one of his contacts in Sydney to do a background check of the great man himself. One of the skeletons in his closet had come to life. The image of an old black and white B movie flashed in front of him. A dusty skeleton emerging from an antique cupboard and chasing him down endless hallways. He smiled and leaned his forearms on the balcony railing. There was no use worrying about the whole thing tonight. Ally and Nicholas were safe. Tomorrow he would start digging. Investigating the kidnapper. He had a name now.

Consciously erasing the deep frown lines on his forehead, Jim let the ocean work its calming magic on his soul. It was a perfect night with the barest hint of a breeze. The sky was a deep, luminous black, shot through with thousands of sparkling stars. It touched the inky sea at the distant horizon somewhere in the darkness.

Gently rolling breakers tumbled onto the white sand illuminated by the lights of Noosa. Here and there couples wandered intertwined and groups of fishermen with lanterns waited for their catch. How long he stood there, he couldn't afterwards remember. Hearing a soft footfall behind him, he straightened and turned to find Ally silhouetted against the light. The demure nightgown she was wearing had turned into a shimmering translucent veil. She was naked underneath it. Desire uncoiled inside him and he stood still, not trusting himself to speak.

Ally walked toward him, not daring to breathe. Now that the moment she was waiting for had come, she felt a stumbling uncertainty. Except for Luke, she had no experience with men. As a shy, mousy teenager, she had been almost invisible to the boys she went to school with. Even the most extroverted class comedians never bothered to turn the charm on for her and she carried that hurt into adult life, even as she blossomed into beauty. Her memories made her secretly insecure as an attractive woman and even when men expressed interest in her, she shied away, not wanting to interact with them, knowing that if they knew the person she really was, they would not even see her. Luke had been different. He and Ally joked that they were as comfortable together as a pair of old slippers.

Whatever she felt for Jim, it wasn't a comfortable feeling. They had met in such unusual circumstances that she didn't react to him with her usual reserve and by the time she became aware of how deeply she felt for him, they had already formed a friendship of sorts. She was able to act casually around him even though her insides were somersaulting.

When she was close enough to touch him, she stopped. Looking up, she couldn't read the expression in his eyes which had darkened to a smouldering charcoal in the dim light of the balcony.

"Nicky is sleeping like a baby." Her voice carried like music on the breeze.

"He should sleep for hours," Jim heard himself say, but his entire attention was focussed on the way Ally moved, and how beautiful she was. She was so near him that he could feel the heat of her body through the thin cotton of the nightgown. He cleared his throat. This was it. Time to end his deception. "Ally, there is something I have to tell you about myself."

Ally smiled in the dim light. He was ready to confide in her. "I'd love to hear it, but later, please, Jim. There is something I have to tell you first. I want to thank you," she whispered on a sigh, "Thank you for my son."

Jim wanted to say that he didn't want her gratitude, but her forgiveness and her love. He leaned imperceptibly nearer. "Don't you know by now that I would do anything for you Ally?"

She nodded as his wind cooled lips touched hers, so gently that tears sprang into her eyes. It felt so right, so perfect. It was as if both their destinies had collided for this moment alone.

Ally touched his cheek with her fingertips, tracing the crease that ran down it when he smiled, delighting in the feel of his beard roughened skin, before threading her fingers through his crisp hair and pulling his head down as their kiss deepened into molten passion.

Wondering at her earlier hesitation, she gave herself fully to him. And took everything he gave. The firm pressure of his mouth on hers answered a clamouring of a thousand nerve endings throughout her body until she could feel nothing else. Her knees grew weak with wanting and would have given way altogether if Jim hadn't gathered her into his arms and carried her into his room.

Ally had never before felt such an almost painful intensity of desire before. Jim carried her on an ever-increasing wave of passion and she clung to him, knowing she would drown if she let him go. She felt a desperation in him as if he was storing up a lifetime of memories in one night, as if he was trying to learn everything about her. What made her cry out, or sigh, or tremble. As if this was the last, as well as the first time he would ever make love to her.

Later, Ally held him tightly until he fell asleep. She felt fiercely protective of this man who was so strong and confident when he was awake. In the moonlight, his sleeping face looked defenceless and vulnerable. As defenceless as her little Nicky. Hating to leave, she nevertheless eased away gently, slipped into her nightgown and crept into her own room. Nicky had not moved. Hopefully he was too young for the ordeal he had been through to leave any permanent scars. Ally got into the bed. The cold sheets gave her a momentary pause to regret leaving Jim's side, she had not slept beside a man for a long time, but now she needed to be close to her baby. To protect him from the world.

She was in the carpark again. Two dark suited men were chasing her. She was trying to run away, but the bitumen was melting and her feet were stuck. She looked down to see Nicky falling away from her and merging with the bitumen. An old man was laughing in her face. In the shadows another man watched on.

"Jim!" she screamed in horror. "Help me!"

But it was not Jim. It was a man with a golden mane and the face of a lion. She shrank back from him and snarled, "You can't escape me. I'm everywhere. So just take it easy. Take it easy."

"Take it easy, Ally. It's only a dream." Jim's warm sleepy voice sounded in her ear."

"Nicky!" she was up and out of the bed in an instant, running to the cot. The cot was silent and empty. "Jim, he's gone, he's g..." then she remembered. She hadn't put Nicholas in the cot. Feeling relieved and foolish and frightened all at the same time, Ally turned back to the bed. Nicky had scooted down to the foot of the bed and lay there on the edge curled around his teddy. Heaving a sigh of relief, she lifted him gently into the cot so he wouldn't fall out. And she wouldn't hurt him in the throes of another nightmare. Nicky grunted but kept sleeping. Jim wrapped his arm around her shoulders as they stood over the cot. Ally was sure she would never forget this moment as long as she lived.

"After what you two have been through, you can't expect to return to normal without a few nightmares." Jim whispered, pulling her closer.

"I dreamt they were taking him again," Ally whispered back, not taking her eyes off Nicholas. "And there was someone else there. A lion man who was everywhere was taunting me."

Jim frowned. A lion man. Max, with his golden mane. That's what they called him. The lion. He had the cunning and the power and the predatory skills. The man he still worked for. Ally was right, the lion man was everywhere. Even in this room. He had to tell her.

Taking a deep breath, he looked down at her drawn and pale face. Not the kind of news she could take at 3am. She had been through too much and she needed to rest. He would tell her tomorrow.

Ally allowed Jim to tuck her in as if she was only a baby too. He looked so tired. After spending the entire day driving and searching, not to mention fighting and getting woken up by her nightmares, it was no surprise.

She put a trembling hand on his arm as he made to move away. "Please don't leave. There's plenty of room in here."

"Are you sure?"

"Yes, yes I'm sure."

Jim had already done something tonight that he had never done before. He had fallen asleep beside another human being. There had been no locked doors between them. His subconscious had let him trust Ally with his rest. He had been completely exhausted at the time. But could he do it again? He was afraid he would crush her, but their bodies melded together perfectly and he found himself drifting off peacefully.

Nicky woke with a sharp note of panic in his cry and Ally scooped him up and hugged him to her before she had even woken up. "Oh, my poor baby, did you have a nasty dream too?"

Dim morning light showed through the filmy curtains that swayed in the breeze and after she had fed and changed him, she sat on the balcony and watched the sun rise as he slept on her chest. Never again would she grumble when she had to wake up early to be with her little boy. Even as her body cried out for rest, her heart rejoiced for Nicky and the happiness she had found with Jim.

CHAPTER SIX

Friday 23 September

Noosa

Blazing sunshine falling across her face woke her hours later, still sitting on an outdoor lounge clutching Nicholas. A gentle breeze ruffled her hair as she stood up stiffly. Nicky woke up and this time he was his usual cuddly happy self before climbing down and running back into the suite. By the time she had followed him in, Jim was pouring cereal into a bowl and attempting to feed Nicky amid bursts of laughter from the little boy as the gooey mess spattered on the table and floor. Jim looked completely out of his depth as he looked up and mouthed HELP. Ally laughed with them as she picked up a cloth to clean up. She couldn't find it in her heart to be even the slightest bit annoyed. It was so good to hear her son's happy voice.

They spent an idyllic morning playing on the sand and wading in the shallows where children of all ages squealed and splashed about. After lunch Nicky readily agreed to a nap. The fresh air, sunshine and water had made him contented and sleepy.

Jim was standing, waiting for her in the lounge. He was wearing a casual polo and still looked cool and collected. Barefoot, Ally found herself level with his collarbone. Smooth tanned skin showed at his throat. She raised herself on tip toes and pressed her lips to his, "I don't think we should waste any more time, do you?" she murmured against his mouth while she touched his cheek.

He grinned, "No ma'am, I certainly do not," as he captured her hand and intertwined his fingers with hers. His smile faded, leaving a serious intensity in his gaze. How could he take advantage of her again, make love to her under false pretences? Jim closed his eyes and bent his head until his forehead touched the smooth skin of her brow. If he told her now, she would leave him. Then the light in his life would vanish, leaving it bleak and lonely. The thought of it almost made him sick.

Ally felt his withdrawal even though he had not moved a muscle. Something was wrong. Very wrong. Was it over? He had helped her when she needed him most. Did he want to leave now? Last night she had been sure he cared for her deeply, but even then, something had been wrong. That desperation she had sensed in him as though his time was running out.

Maybe he was afraid of hurting her feelings and was trying to let her down gently. Well, she would make it easy for him, let him off the hook.

"You don't want to?" she asked, pulling away to look at him, searching his face for the answer.

For the life of him, he couldn't find anything to say. She looked so hurt and uncertain, standing there in front of him, and he loved her so much. Jim ran the scenario over again, looking for answers. If he told her now, she would leave. If she left, he couldn't protect her and Nicky. The spectre of the person who had hired kidnappers and had them killed, hung over them, vaguely threatening. He couldn't tell her yet. It was still too dangerous.

He knew he was just inventing excuses, but they sounded valid, didn't they? Anything to let him stay, just a few more days.

"You have no idea how much I want to," he said hoarsely, bending his head to hers and demolishing her doubts with a single searing kiss.

Afterwards, Jim pulled up the sheet to cover them. She was the most beautiful woman he'd ever seen as she leaned on her elbow, tucking the sheet around her. "I've never felt like this before," she whispered. "It's..." she searched for the right words. "It's so strong that sometimes I think I'm going to die because my heart clenches so tight. Stop. You make me forget to breathe when you look at me like that. I'm a little afraid of the feelings you awaken in me."

Jim smiled and hugged her tightly, afraid to speak.

CHAPTER SEVEN

Saturday 24 September

Jim looked up from the book he was reading to watch Ally and Nicholas playing with a set of giant blocks on the floor. The toddler was delighting in demolishing the towers as soon as Ally built them. Jim was amazed at her patience. He would have given up after the first two structures had been flattened.

Listening to the bursts of gurgling laughter, he realized that the towers were not in themselves important, rather a means to an end – the youngster's enjoyment. Ally's mock scolding added to the merriment. She looked up at Jim and smiled in exasperation, "this isn't fair, you know. Come down here and help for goodness' sake."

Without a second's notice, she reached up and pulled him down to the floor, handing him a pile of blocks and laughing. "It's your turn."

Feeling strangely out of place, Jim began to stack the blocks. They were lighter than he expected. Searching through his memory, he honestly couldn't recall ever playing with blocks during his childhood. This would be a long overdue learning experience.

Before long a strange sense of calm and contentment stole over him, sitting there on the floor, playing like a child, laughing with Nicky as the blocks tumbled to the floor. He found himself enjoying the fall even more than the construction.

Ally smiled to herself. It was good to see him doing something silly. Nicky laughed even more when he managed to topple Jim's highest tower and Jim had let his lower lip droop sulkily. She just couldn't figure out how he could look so attractive sitting on the floor, completely out of his element, but so natural.

"I was thinking of taking you and Nicky to Underwater World today," he remembered when the little boy had tired of the game. "But we'll have to leave fairly soon before the roads get too congested with weekend traffic."

"Great," Ally agreed, scooping Nicky up and heading for her room. She stood for several minutes in front of the now well stocked closet. There were so many gorgeous clothes to choose from, that she was tempted to say she had nothing to wear.

Finally, she decided on some tailored linen shorts and a soft peach coloured blouse that complemented Nicholas' more colourful version of her outfit. Her purse fit neatly into her large pocket and she slung Nicholas' mint coloured nappy bag over one shoulder before picking up and hugging him. They looked in the mirror together, admiring the finished effect. Their eyes met in the reflection and tears welled in her eyes as she realised how lucky she was to have him back. Giving him a quick kiss on the forehead, she spun around and joined Jim.

"You must show me the store where you bought all of these beautiful clothes. I love to shop," she added dreamily as they drove through the low-lying scrubland between Noosa and Mooloolaba. "Between work and looking after Nicky, I haven't been shopping for ages."

"They don't have stores around here, only fashion boutiques," he replied with a smile. "To be perfectly honest though, the concierge organised it all, I have no experience buying women's or kid's clothes."

Ally smiled back at him, itching to tell him how amazing he looked today in his light grey jacket that barely covered the shoulder holster she knew he had on. The peaceful part of her rejected the idea of the violence that the gun he carried represented, but the protective mother in her was still traumatized by how defenceless she had been at the airport, just a few short days ago and didn't mind at all. She sighed and looked out of the window in time to see the road lift onto a headland and the magnificence of the Pacific Ocean spread out before her as far as the eye could see before the road dipped again.

In less than an hour they had arrived at the Mooloolaba Spit, a long finger of land stretching into the sea. A beautiful wharf had been built next to it, home to dozens of quaint and colourful craft shops, restaurants and art galleries specializing in all things nautical as well as the Oceanarium which was their destination.

They decided to have lunch first. Trying to choose a restaurant was no easy task. There were small dark and cosy coffee shops, boisterous family restaurants teeming with holidaymakers, fish and chip shops and swanky black-tie establishments.

Finally, they settled on a restaurant that floated on the water and looked and felt like the interior of an old sailing ship. Nets hung from the ceiling, trapping colourful wooden fish in their folds and a rickety staircase led to an authentic looking mess hall. Each table held a weathered glass bottle filled with the dried grasses that grow on sand dunes next to the sea and an old fashioned, glowing hurricane lamp. Jim ordered the fisherman's basket and soon they were enjoying a huge platter of crumbed fish fillets, crab, prawns and chips, washed down with fresh lemonade.

After lunch they made their way slowly to the Oceanarium. Nicky was tired after lunch, so Jim carried him on his hip. On the way, Ally spotted a little shop selling sea shells and pulled Jim and Nicky inside. The young sales assistant was dressed fashionably in a simple sand coloured dress, liberally adorned with shell jewellery. Gorgeous drop earrings and pendant vied for attention with an elaborate rope and clamshell belt.

"Hi!" she beamed enthusiastically at the trio, "what an adorable little boy you have."

"Thank you," Jim and Ally replied in unison, laughing easily.

"Are you planning a baby sister or brother for him?" the girl asked innocently. "You are such a good-looking couple."

Ally and Jim looked at each other for a long moment.

"That sounds like a brilliant idea," he said, not taking his eyes off Ally. She grew warm from the intensity of his gaze and nodded.

The sales assistant coughed politely. "How can I help you?"

"I'd like to buy that shell," Ally replied, impulsively pointing to the window. Then she laughed. The window was completely obscured with shells and coral. "This one just here," she chose at random.

It was a beautiful soft, pearly apricot shade inside, with wickedly jagged, cream and brown spines covering the exterior. When she held it up to her ear, she could hear the whoosh of the sea from its depths. She let Nicky listen too.

"Here, let me wrap it up for you," the girl offered, pulling out a sheet of shell patterned tissue paper, adding, "you'll have to be careful of these spines, they are pretty sharp."

Ally paid for her purchase and put in into her pocket. Linking her arm through Jim's free one, she hummed happily as they entered the dark, cavernous foyer of the Oceanarium.

It greeted them with a multitude of wondrous sights. Walls of illuminated jelly fish provided an eerie entry into the tropical room, teeming with exotic fish and swaying coral. Nicholas' eyes grew wide as Jim hoisted him onto his shoulders for a closer look at a lacy Angel fish that floated through its tank like a feather in the wind. They grew wider still as a groper popped out of his lair and snatched a bit of food that was travelling on the current.

Rounding the first corner, they found a large open wading pool. A group of small children had gathered at the edges. Ally leant over the have a closer look. An attendant was carefully scooping out a lobster for the children to touch. Jim brought Nicholas down for his turn, but Nicky buried his face into Jim's shoulder, moaning fearfully. Ally rubbed his little back reassuringly. The onslaught of sensory stimulation was probably too much already, without having to touch any strange looking creatures.

"It's ok, my sweetheart," she whispered to him. "You don't have to pat him if you don't want to."

Hearing her voice, Nicholas turned to her, arms outstretched.

"Oh, my darling little baby," she sighed as she hugged him tightly.

Afterwards, she could never exactly remember when the feeling returned. The feeling of being watched, of hostile eyes staring from the shadows. It could have been right there, near the wading pool, when she had held Nicholas and felt it was too good to be true. Her baby safe in her arms. The man she loved beside her. A decent, honest, honourable man who had saved her little boy from goodness only knows what terrors. A vague disquiet edged into her contentment. She was just being silly. Struggling to ignore the feeling, she left the wading pool, still holding Nicholas safe against her side, while Jim walked beside them, nappy bag over his shoulder like any other dad. Ally smiled contentedly.

Further along, the darkened corridors branched into three. An illuminated sign showed the way to the seal pool, the fresh water river and, down the stairs, the main attraction, an underwater walk-through tunnel. Jim glanced at his watch, then at the sign.

"We have exactly half an hour before the next seal demonstration. Just enough time to look at the tunnel. What do you think?"

"I might just have enough energy for that," Ally smiled feeling Nicky relaxing and growing heavy in her arms.

As they stepped onto the downward staircase behind several other people, Ally saw a sudden flash of movement behind her. She spun to look and almost overbalanced on the step. Besides normal, innocent looking families like theirs, she could see nothing. Nevertheless, she tightened her grip on Nicholas. Fear displaced any tiredness she felt carrying him.

"What is it?" she heard Jim's concerned voice near her ear.

"Probably nothing," she shrugged mustering up some semblance of calm. "I just thought I saw something in the shadows. Paranoia is a hard habit to break."

"This place is a bit spooky," Jim sympathised, adding, "I sure wouldn't like to be stranded here after closing time. The cleaners must have nerves of steel."

Ally was grateful for his understanding and that he hadn't ridiculed her fears. The underwater tunnel was almost overwhelming. With its invisible curving acrylic walls and ceiling, it was like stepping into the deep ocean. Schools of silver Trevally swam silently beside and above them. Gropers and eels peered out of their hiding places in the rocks. Small fish that Ally didn't recognise darted in and out of the wavy corals. Several sharks cruised among the smaller fish, ignoring them, their tiny, expressionless eyes intent on something just out of range.

Jim took Nicky from Ally and handed her the nappy bag. The little boy was overjoyed at the moving shapes and strange creatures. His eyebrows moved higher in that beautiful expression of wonder children have and seeing his evident happiness, Ally relaxed and gave herself over to the experience.

The centre of the tunnel floor moved slowly forward like a conveyor belt and a steady stream of people glided along it. Some stepped off to take a closer look, as did Jim and Ally when they saw a black ray which slept motionless on the sandy bottom.

Subconsciously, Ally noted that someone else had stepped off exactly when they did and was standing behind her. It was an uncomfortable experience. Casually, she moved around so she could still listen to Jim, but also glance over his shoulder. A tall, thin man in faded jeans and a soiled T-shirt stood a few feet away from them, looking away so she couldn't quite see his face. Several tourists stepped between them and when they stepped back onto the conveyor, the man had gone. He hadn't moved past them. Ally was sure of it. She shivered, and it had nothing to do with the temperature.

Determinedly, she tried to regain her contentment and enthusiasm. Nevertheless, when the conveyor deposited them at the end of the tunnel, she breathed a giant sigh of relief.

The crowd dispersed, leaving a relatively free, carpeted walkway in front of them. As they walked along the corridor, the dark walls seemed to be closing in on them, narrowing ever so slightly. The fish in their tanks on one side watched the humans with impassive, unblinking eyes as their mouths opened and closed in silent screams. Ally was sure that the tiny blue flecks in the carpet were about to leap up and attack her.

"Oh, let's go look at those seals now," she gasped. Nothing had happened in the tunnel but she couldn't shake the dread that enveloped her. Something was wrong.

Jim checked his watch again, "Definitely, it's almost time," he agreed.

The seals proved to be a welcome change. Their pool was under a light and airy dome that let filtered sunlight in. Despite the heat and humidity, Ally could breathe more easily here, in the daylight, with animals which were obviously of her world, frolicking in the water. They were mammals after all and proved it by coming up for air with loud snorts and calling to each other in raucous, happy voices. Older fur seals reclined lazily on the rocks that were part of a display behind the main pool. A glass fence stopped some of the splashing water, but not all. Rows of seats rose up like those in an auditorium. Luckily, the ones in the front were still mainly empty and Ally headed for the front row where they had room to change Nicky and feed him his bottle.

Soon after, Jim nudged her quietly. Nicky was sound asleep on his shoulder. The peaceful expression on his dear little face brought tears to her eyes. When would she stop worrying about him? Probably never, a voice in her head replied. She pulled a soft rug from the bag and spread it on the seats between them. Jim gently placed Nicky on the rug, smoothing his hair back from his forehead with an unconsciously caring gesture. Ally was certain he wasn't even aware of what he had done.

She thought she was falling in love with him. Now, she was sure. She closed her fingers over his strong hand and held it tightly. "I love you," she whispered impulsively. The words had just come out, unplanned, unrehearsed, but when she heard herself saying then, she knew it was true.

Jim's dark head jerked up. Ally read an answering love in his eyes momentarily, before the light when out of them, to be replaced by some other emotion. Something darker that she did not recognise or understand and that made her scared.

"I..." he began, but at that moment, with a clash of cymbals, the show began. Reluctantly, Ally looked away, but that look on his face stayed with her.

It was not exactly a show, rather the seals demonstrated their ability with a playful joy and enthusiasm. The trainer fed them numerous quantities of small fish as they dived, played with colourful balls and leapt high out of the water. He explained that each of the behaviours was common in the wild. Ally laughed with delight at their antics. Enjoyment was evident in every line of their sleek bodies. All through the noise, the splashing, the loudspeaker commentary, the laughter and the clapping, Nicholas slept as if he was in his own cot.

All too soon it was over. Most of the audience left, while others arrived to watch the seals, which, well fed and happy, continued to play and snort. Nicky woke from his nap a short time later completely unfazed at the strange environment.

"Og," he said, pointing to the seals.

"Seals," Ally told him. "But they look like dogs. Aren't they lovely seals?"

"Eals," Nicholas repeated seriously, without taking his eyes off them.

"Time to finish your bottle," Ally said, pulling it out of the bag. Being a big boy and no longer tired, he fed himself and was soon drinking contentedly. Jim was fascinated at how much the toddler moved while he drank his milk. His legs kicked slowly in the air, his toes curled and uncurled in his tiny sandals and his hands were busy playing with the bottle as it emptied into bubbles.

Less than a week ago, if anyone had told Jim that he would be so captivated by a baby, he would have scoffed and said "Never!" He smiled to himself. Was he getting ready to settle down? Maybe it was just this baby. Maybe it was this baby's mother. He had found the perfect woman after all, and she loved him. They would be able to give Nicholas a loving, happy home life, something Jim had craved his entire life. You're getting ahead of yourself Conrad, he told himself. He was sure of his own feelings, but what about Ally? She had only just met him. She knew nothing about him. Did she really love him, or was it just gratitude, a vulnerable woman, responding to the man who had helped her in a desperate and dramatic moment?

Was it a love that would stand up to a challenge? Jim hoped so, but he wasn't sure. Unfortunately, it wouldn't be long before he found out. Would she still feel the same when she knew the whole truth about him?

Almost too soon, it was time to return to their hotel. They would be returning to Brisbane in the morning, the holiday would be over. Secretly, they were both looking forward to being home, together, with Nicky safe. Ally had to work on her paranoid overactive imagination though.

"I have to stop by the Ladies on the way out," she laughed as she carried Nicky with her into the change room. Without Jim helping, Nicky decided not to cooperate with his nappy change. He kicked and twisted and all but rolled off the narrow change table. After his short nap, his energy was abundant. As Ally struggled with the squirming little boy, her hair fell about her face in disarray. No one would have believed that she had been doing this for over a year, she though wryly as she straightened, looked at her flustered face in the mirror. Luckily, there was no one in the room to see the fun.

Nicholas certainly thought it was fun. He was giggling and squealing with joy at making his mother look like a chump.

"Oh, you little rascal!" Ally mock scolded him. "We're almost finished and then we can go for a nice drive. Come on now." The closed toilet door in the corner of the room Ally hadn't noticed before, started to creak open behind her. Ally looked up, mesmerised, watching the slow swing of the door in the mirror.

"Mama!" Nicholas protested at the lack of attention. Ally straightened his pants and picked him up, holding him tightly without taking her eyes off the mirror. As if in slow motion, a man stepped into the room. Even before she saw him, she knew. It was the scruffy looking man in the dirty t-shirt. He had a baseball cap pulled low over his head. The man who she had seen in the underwater tunnel. Her instincts had not been wrong. It was a pity she hadn't trusted them though.

The man raised his head with an almost deliberate slowness and she caught the full impact of his ice blue eyes. It was Julian Roche. The kidnapper and murderer. His glare fastened greedily on Nicky. Even as her brain registered the impossibility of what she was seeing, he laughed coldly.

"Thought you were safe, didn't you?" He spoke in a cultured, educated voice at odds with his current disguise. "Thought they could hold me in one of their inadequate holding cells? Hardly, my dear."

Ally thought frantically. He was between her and the door. If she and Nicholas tried to run, he would catch them easily. If she called for help, he would reach her before Jim had even heard her. What was she to do? At least Julian didn't have a gun pointed at her, which didn't necessarily mean he was unarmed. Anyway, he looked like he could kill them both with his bare hands without raising a sweat.

The kidnapper smiled with enjoyment. He was reading her mind. "No way out, Mrs Reed?" he asked with mock solicitude.

"W...why?" she stammered, real fear tightening her vocal cords. "Why are you doing this to us? I don't have very much money."

"I don't want or need your money," he replied, pausing and emphasising the 'your'. "You really are a stupid woman Mrs Reed. If you have not yet met your adversary, it is not for me to spoil the surprise." The man swaggered closer. He was enjoying her fear, feeding his ego with it, becoming even more confident.

"Why do you want my baby?" Ally persisted. She needed to find a weapon. Her hand reached slowly into the nappy bag and encountered a bottle of powder that she never used but was a present from Louise. "Why have you gone to all this trouble?" Her fingers twisted the lid. It wouldn't come off. She worked at it, trying to keep her expression neutral.

If Julian noticed her movements, he gave no sign. "It is not I who wants this child." His mouth twitched from the effort it took not to tell her the truth. The surprise on her face would be almost worth giving the game away. "But I do have a score to settle with you."

"Me?" Ally squeaked, astonished. Who had wanted Nicholas then, Max Reed after all? She had thought it was over. She had been living in a paradise of self-delusion.

"I do not like to be thwarted or laughed at or beaten." The kidnapper continued. "And I will not let that go unpunished."

Ally's blood ran cold. She knew for certain that he meant every word. Her fingers tugged at the lid harder, and finally with a tiny pop it came off.

"Well," he moved even closer, almost close enough. "I shall have to kill you, my dear lady. It won't hurt terribly much, because I'm really good at it. Unless you irritate me even more."

"And my baby?" She had to keep him talking.

"What do you think I am, a monster? Just put him down and leave him." Julian didn't really believe that a mother like Alexandria Reed would leave her baby, despite his reassuring words. She would protect the little boy with her dying breath. He tried anyway. It would make the task less messy. There was one thing Julian hated, it was untidiness. "I'm sure his squawks

177

will alert your friend to his need for company. If you do not, however, I will have no compunction to break the brat's neck."

"I gather you didn't have a very pleasant trip with him," Ally sneered, baiting him, urging him closer.

"I would rather babysit eels," he lied. "So, put him down! Now, before I get upset!" His white smooth-skinned hands reached towards Nicholas. At that moment, someone knocked on the door.

"Ally, are you ok in there?" Jim asked.

Julian Roche's eyes narrowed. He stopped in mid step and turned towards the sound. It was all the distraction Ally needed. She whirled around, still clutching Nicholas one handed and flung the contents of the powder tin into Julian's face. As he roared with anger and brought his hand up to rub the tiny particles from his eyes, she shoved past him and bolted for the door.

He recovered quickly and started after her, but Jim had already opened the door. Hoping the kidnapper had told her the truth about not wanting Nicky, she thrust the little boy into Jim's arms, ignoring his questions, and ran back into the darkened display corridors as fast as she could. Why she didn't stay and let Jim protect them both she never knew. She thought only of leading the danger away from her child. Her own safety was secondary. A forgotten instinct that causes the mother bird to limp away from its nest full of chicks took over. She wanted the predator after her and her alone.

People scattered before her wild-eyed flight. A path would open up for her at the last second as she wove around them. No one tried to help her, but at least they didn't try to stop either. She tripped over someone's foot, but caught herself before she fell, and raced on. He was following her. She could hear that he was close behind. Shouted curses followed her and echoed hollowly off the walls.

She ran deeper into the maze of corridors, hoping to lose him, but it was no use. He was gaining, his footsteps thudding dully on the carpet. Ally was panting now. She couldn't keep up this pace for much longer. There were fewer people here too. Parts of the corridor were empty. None of the tourists would have been able to help her anyway. All they had done was get in the way.

Despite her fear, Ally was glad. If he was after her, that meant Nicky was safe with Jim. Jim would look after her little boy even if something happened to her. She was sure of it.

Gathering her remaining strength, she sprinted around a corner and dived into a doorway marked STAFF ONLY, NO ADMITTANCE. She found herself in almost pitch darkness, a narrow passageway. Feeling her way forward along the wall, she fought to still her breathing. A stitch in her side needled, she hated running.

The sound of droning machinery urged her forward. The passageway angled to the left, then opened into a massive room. Rows of gauges lined the walls. Cylindrical pumps the size of a small car cycled fresh sea water into a water tank as big as an Olympic pool. The edge of the tank was waist high and made of grey concrete. The entire room seemed to be grey. There was no one else there, the machinery was running automatically.

Ally leant on the edge of the water tank, trying to catch her breath. The briny smell of salt water and humidity assailed her nostrils. She was right above the underwater tunnel. Dozens of fish swam in the fast-flowing current. The sharks looked even bigger from above. Far below, she could see distorted figures of people, gliding under the water through the tunnel, oblivious to her plight.

The loud, steady hum of the pumps drowned out all other sound. She didn't hear Julian Roche until he was less than an arm's length away. She smelt his sickly-sweet scent, cutting through the brine.

"Ah," he whispered into her ear, "how perfect m'dear. You do like to make things easier for me, don't you? I will enlist the help of my counterparts from the deep to terminate you." And with that, he ran his hand lightly across her neck. A sharp pain followed his touch and Ally saw drops of dark red blood swirl into the water below her. Reaching her hand up, she encountered a warm stickiness at her throat. He had cut her. Not deeply enough to cut an artery or vein, to kill her quickly, but deep enough.

Like so many ships returning to the same homing beacon, the sharks in the water tank had turned from their ceaseless circuit of the pool and were following the trail of blood to its source.

Ally pressed her hand tightly to the wound, trying to stem the flow and pulled back from the water, but Julian had grasped the back of her neck and pushed her head inexorably closer to the water's edge. Her breath came in gasps as Ally raised her arms to prise his hand away, but they were wet with blood and slid off.

Ally prayed that Jim would come and save her, like the hero did in an old movie, but deep down, she knew that he would never find her in time. This was probably the end and it was all her fault. She should have stayed with him and they could have made a stand. She should never have run away from the safety of his arms like an idiot. Julian was right. She made it all too easy for him.

Sensing her despair, Julian slammed her into the barrier. She cried out as her hip met the wall. Then she remembered. The shell! The shell she had bought what seemed a lifetime ago. The shell with sharp spines and hard edges. Hope flared. First, she had to get him to loosen his grip. Sagging heavily against the wall, she feigned resignation. She hung over the water limply as if defeated. Dimly, she could see that some of the tourists had noticed the drama above them and were pointing up. Surely someone would summon help before it was too late.

The sharks were at the surface now, circling in the enclosed space, their sleek grey flanks almost touching each other. Triangular fins broke the surface and water swished as the awesome creatures grew excited at the thought of a second lunch. The thought made Ally relax and think more clearly.

She let her hands drop to her sides and was rewarded by a loosening of the pressure on the back of her head. In a heartbeat, they would reach her. Not wasting another second, she slid her hand into her pocket and felt the spiky shell, grateful that she hadn't put it in her bag.

Julian must have believed that the fight had gone out of her as he jerked her upright and swung her to face him.

Waves of dizziness assailed her as her head lifted. She must have lost more blood than she thought. Unable to hold herself up, she started to collapse.

"No, you don't," he snarled. "I want you awake." His fingers dug mercilessly into the softness of her shoulders. Even as she flinched from the pain, a part of her brain registered that he must have put away the knife. There was still a chance. She looked into his eyes and saw pure enjoyment in their pale gleam. This man loved to kill.

"I bet you loved pulling the wings off flies when you were a kid," she choked out.

"Actually, I preferred impaling them with a hot pin. I could watch the life drain out of them that way. Ahh, sweet memories. You really are an amusing woman. It is a pity to end it this way. I'm starting to like you. But," he sighed dramatically, "you've just been too much trouble."

"Anything worth having in life is too much trouble," Ally replied, her words slurring, blinking back the familiar darkness of unconsciousness. Not now, she told her brain. Don't fail me again. Stay awake for just a few more seconds. "Don't you agree?" Slowly, as she spoke, she pulled the shell, still wrapped in tissue paper out of her pocket.

"You may be right. There is something I want that I am going to a great deal of trouble for right now. Soon I will have it all. This is goodbye dear lady. I have loved watching you die."

"I don't think so," Ally mumbled as she concentrated all of her remaining strength into the hand with the shell and swung it as hard as she could into his cheek. When she felt it strike his cheekbone, she increased the pressure and raked it across his face.

If she wasn't so appalled at her own violence, and the power she derived from it, she would have laughed at the amazed and horrified look in his eyes. Three lines of blood welled across his cheek and nose.

"That's for the flies," she ground out as brought her foot up and kicked him in the shin. "Didn't anyone ever tell you not to mess with a mother bear's cub?"

The fingers on her shoulders clenched spasmodically and released as she drove her elbow into his ribs. For long seconds he stepped back gasping before the knife flashed in his hand. Even as she looked at him fatalistically, head swimming, waiting for the end, she felt proud that she had put up a fight. She wished she had worked out more, maybe taken kickboxing lessons, or karate. Then again, it was never too late to start. She had to do it now, before he fully recovered from the shock of her defence.

Supporting herself with one hand on the concrete wall, she kicked hard at the wrist holding the knife, and was rewarded by the sound of it clattering to the floor. Then, as he reached down for it, she kicked him again for good measure, square in the face. Blood spurted from his nose. That straight, thin, aristocratic nose looked like a twisted pop art tap. The eyes above the nose bore into her and she knew that it was not enough. He started to get up.

Shaking off another wave of dizziness, she pushed herself off the wall and stumbled towards the door and freedom. It was so cold in this room. Lucky the big fish in this room weren't tropical, she thought, because this weather was awful. Ally's mind was starting to wander and she wanted to laugh for some reason. She

184

was seeing things that weren't there. She saw Jim, gun drawn. It was only when he stopped, shocked at blood seeping across her chest that she realized that he was real.

She laughed hysterically and collapsed in his arms. "You're a bit late. It's so cold in here."

"Hold on love, you've lost a lot of blood. Let's get you to the hospital."

"What about him?" Ally tried to turn her head, but the pain in her neck was excruciating.

"Where is he?" Jim asked tersely.

"Over near the tank wall," she pointed. Jim helped her turn to look. The kidnapper was gone. Only a small, bloodstained patch on the grey concrete marked the spot where he had lain. Icy dread enveloped her. He could be anywhere. "Oh no, Jim, he's after Nicky!"

"Nicky's safe."

"I have to see him now!" Ally tried to get up and groaned.

"Ok, but you're not walking." With that, he swung her into his arms and carried her through the maze of corridors to the manager's office. True to his word, Jim had kept her baby safely locked in the office with the manager and his assistant, playing happily with a pile of sparkling fish-shaped keyrings, oblivious to the drama surrounding him.

"Thank you," Ally whispered, as Jim set her down on the floor beside Nicky and called the ambulance.

Tears were running freely down her cheeks as she slowly sank down and lost consciousness.

Ally woke in a strange room. The shadows were lengthening on the pale green wall. She lay on a small, surprisingly comfortable bed in the middle of the room. Moving her head gingerly she encountered a bulky dressing on her neck. A faint sting reminded her of the wound there.

Raising her eyes, she saw a grey triangle hanging over the bed, suspended by a buckled strap and if she moved just her eyes to the left, she could just see a drip stand with a bag of dark red fluid hanging from a hook and attaching to a small blue box. She was in the hospital having a transfusion. Ally closed her eyes and listened. The clinking of the dinner trolley moving closer somewhere outside the room interspersed with voices here and there and television sounds. They were the same sounds she heard on the first night she held baby Nicholas in her arms and dozed after a long labour. Comforting, safe sounds. The smell was the same too.

"You're awake Mrs Reed," chimed a cheery voice beside her. A young woman with a pretty pale face framed by reddish curls that struggled to escape from a neat updo smiled down at her. "I'm Chiara, I'll be your nurse this evening. Is there anything you need? Is the cannula comfortable?"

Ally looked at her hazily. The nurse went on, hardly pausing for breath. "This is your second bag of packed cells. You should start feeling better soon."

"Packed cells?"

"Red blood cells, to replenish the blood you lost. You were very pale and cool when you came in."

Ally nodded. The action hurt her throat and she became aware of a sting where the cannula entered the back of her left wrist. Her hand felt cold and sore around the area. A splint was holding her immobilized like a handcuff. She wanted to be free of it. She wanted to see Nicholas.

"My baby?" she tried to sit up and failed.

"Now, don't you worry, Mrs Reed, your little boy is right here."

Chiara helped Ally sit up. Nicky was not more than a metre away, sleeping peacefully in a while hospital cot. Ally sighed with relief and sank back onto the pillows. "Call me Ally," she smiled up at the nurse. "Thank you so much for looking after us."

"Not a problem," the girl beamed. "I love kids. Actually, I'm on loan from Children's ward to special you two. There is a policeman outside the door too, to keep you safe and cosy, so you can relax and recover."

Ally didn't answer. Julian Roche would try again. She was sure of it. After the injuries she had inflicted on him, there would be no stopping him. He would come after them again. Even if the police caught him again, she doubted they could keep him imprisoned.

He was violent to an almost insane degree but also extremely clever and obsessive. And he said he wanted Nicholas. Why, she still didn't know.

What could she do? Ask Jim to run away with her and Nicholas? Change their names maybe. Or stay and fight. To set a trap for the killer. The prey becoming the hunters.

Safe in the hospital room with Nicky sleeping beside her, Ally began to plan.

Jim opened the door to Ally's room softly and tiptoed in. He felt a little silly clutching a large bunch of pink roses in his hand. But his embarrassment fled when he saw Ally lying on the hospital bed in the middle of the room. She looked so pale and fragile. Violet shadows under her eyes contrasted with the whiteness of her skin. Her hair fanned out on the pillow. She must have washed the blood out of it already.

She was asleep, small and vulnerable.

A young nurse emerged from the shadows and with a cheerful wink took the roses from him. He smiled back absently, his attention riveted on Ally. A recliner sat beside the bed and Jim lowered himself into it gratefully. After riding in the ambulance with Ally and Nicky and making sure they were admitted, he had returned to the Oceanarium and helped the police with their investigation.

All they found was some blood and an open emergency fire escape. He still didn't know how the man had been injured. Ally must have put up quite a fight. When she had burst out of the parent's room and thrust Nicky at him, he had been taken aback and the moment's hesitation had allowed a heavily disguised Julian Roche to barrel after her, knocking Jim off balance as he tried to protect Nicholas from the impact.

By the time he had righted himself and made sure Nicholas was unharmed, they had disappeared. The decision not to run after them while holding Nicky had almost cost Ally her life. Fortunately, while he was in the manager's office, one of the employees had rushed in, saying that there was a man and woman struggling above the oceanarium tunnel.

A soft moan from the bed brought Jim back to the present. Ally's hand moved restlessly on the bed. Jim reached over and took her hand in his. She smiled in her sleep and mumbled something unintelligible. Jim kissed her softly on the forehead. As soon as she was released from this hospital, he was taking her as far away as possible. He couldn't live with the thought of Roche attacking her again. He quietly tiptoed out again. She needed her sleep.

Sunday 25 September

Donna came to take Ally's statement the next morning, while Jim took Nicholas for a walk. The blonde policewoman was contrite as she sat at Ally's bedside, tablet in hand. "We should have pulled out

189

all the stops to warn you. We didn't expect Roche to find you so quickly."

"He is a very determined man," Ally observed.

"I'll say. We have linked his fingerprints to an unsolved homicide in Melbourne. The victim was well guarded and had bodyguards and a top-notch security system in place. The calibre bullet, angle of entry, position of the body, also match the bodies in Eidsvold." Donna glanced at Ally. "Oh, I'm sorry, I didn't mean to upset you."

"That's Ok Donna. I'm just glad the net is closing in on him. Seems odd though, that he tried to kill me with a knife this time. Maybe he wanted to give me the personal touch. He looked like he was having a lot of fun seeing how scared he could make me. I don't think he liked having his hair pulled the other night!"

"Sounds reasonable. Men like that don't like to be the ones humiliated and overpowered. I think he underestimated you and Jim Conrad. Once a cop, always a challenge."

"Jim was a policeman?" Ally was shocked. Surely, he would have told her something as significant as that. "Why didn't he tell me?"

Donna shrugged apologetically. "I should have let him tell you himself when he was ready. He and Michael Wilson were partners. It is a shame really."

"Why did he leave? Why did he keep it a secret?"

"When this is over, you should ask him Ally. It really isn't my place."

"Oh no. I have to know! I have to know who I've let into my life. Who is even now alone with my son!"

Donna shrugged. "It isn't like that. It was on the news. Jim Conrad was," she paused to find the right words, "a bright and shining light on the force. He was commended for bravery twice and made the cover of the Police Digest. He trained in hostage negotiation." She sat back in her chair, remembering. "About three years ago, there was a hold up in a Sydney restaurant. Hostages were taken. Jim bargained for the release of the civilians in exchange for himself. When he went in, he found the gunman had not released two of the hostages. One was a waitress and the gunman's ex-girlfriend. Jim had just about convinced him to let them go when one of the sharp shooters took a shot and missed. The gunman retaliated by shooting his ex, and then turning the gun on himself."

Ally wiped tears from her eyes. She remembered the story. It was so pointless and tragic.

Donna continued, "Jim was devastated and angry. Even though the enquiry cleared both officers, he resigned and disappeared for a while. Next time we heard of him, he had set up his own company investigating industrial espionage and fraud. He clearly wasn't going to follow anyone's orders again and probably didn't want to get involved with gunmen and violence again either. Actually, I barely recognised him when I first saw him with you. He was destined to be a great cop."

Or a dead one, Ally thought to herself. No wonder he hadn't told her. How do you bring up something like that?

She remembered the morning he had sat in front of Police Headquarters, waiting for her to finish the press conference. Once he had belonged in a building just like that one and now, he couldn't bring himself to even walk through the doors. He must have been more deeply affected than anyone realized by the shooting. It explained a lot of the things she hadn't understood about him.

The policeman who had found the tiny baby boy in a box and had loved him until the end of his life had instilled a love of the force in that boy. Jim had said that the police station had been a second home to him. He had grown up with heroes and become one himself. Now he was her hero. He had found Nicholas and had saved him, when the entire police force had failed.

She wondered if that was why Luke had called on him to help her, because he knew Jim's true character and knew he could trust him with her and Nicky's life. She felt the familiar stab of guilt that she had been protected, but Luke had faced death alone. Maybe it was like that for Jim too. Maybe he felt guilty that he lived and the hostage died.

Ally was certain that when he was ready, he would tell her and let her share his grief as she had shared hers. On that optimistic thought, she fell asleep and was still sleeping soundly when Jim and Nicky came back. She looked a little better, Jim thought, not only her colour, which was returning, but she looked happier, even in sleep.

One of the nurses came in and offered to feed Nicky but, taking one look at the trusting little face, Jim decided he would try and do it himself. The nappy change proved challenging as Jim had no experience with the wriggling, leg waving routine little ones performed when free of clothing, but he managed it somehow, and was happy there was no audience. By the time he had finished fastening it, the nurse had returned with a delicious kid's meal and Nicky ate hungrily before finishing off a cup of milk. After the big day the little boy was exhausted and when Jim picked him up, he yawned and his sandy head began to droop onto Jim's shoulder. Placing him carefully into his cot and patting his back, Jim wondered if he should be singing a lullaby or something. The problem was, he didn't know any lullabies, so he leant over the cot and sang "Born to be Wild" very softly. It was the only song he could think of. Before he had finished the second verse, Nicky's eyelids had closed and he slept, completely relaxed.

The phone buzzed in his pocket and he picked it up hurriedly, before it woke Ally, and moved into the corner of the room.

"Hey, big buddy, what are you up to?" Michael Wilson's voice boomed in his ear.

"Mike, good to hear from you. You wouldn't believe it if I told you." Jim spoke softly into the phone.

"Try me."

"I've been changing nappies and putting a baby to sleep, successfully I might add."

"You're right Conrad. I don't believe you. I thought you didn't like kids."

"I thought I didn't too. Guess it depends on the kid. What gives?"

"I just heard what that creep tried to do to Ally. Is she ok?"

"He sliced her throat and tried to feed her to some sharks, but otherwise she's great." Jim tried to keep his voice casual, but his friend knew him too well.

"You two seemed to be hitting it off rather well when I saw you last." Mike made it sound like a question.

"Stop fishing, Mike." Jim glanced over at Ally. Her back was to him, so he didn't know if she was still asleep or not, but he had no intention of explaining his feeling for her with anyone, friend or not.

"Have you told her who you're working for?" Mike changed the subject.

"No, not yet." Jim frowned. Michael had a knack for asking him just the sort of question he didn't want to examine too closely himself.

"I wouldn't put it off if I were you, big buddy, it could lead to a real sticky situation."

Ally was starting to stir.

"I know it. Look I have to go, Ally's just waking up. Thanks for the call, and for your help in Eidsvold."

"Glad to do it. Gets a bit dull around here sometimes, and after that little episode of excitement, I'm thinking of requesting a transfer back to Brisbane."

"Let me know when it comes through, we can talk over old times." Jim looked over at Ally and found her smiling at him through her sleep mussed hair.

Wasting no more time, Jim ended the call and walked over to her bedside. "You looked so happy while you are sleeping. Beautiful too."

"Actually, I was dreaming about you and me and lots and lots of bubbles," she laughed.

"Intriguing," he grinned back. "But seriously, we have to make a plan. We've got to get you and Nicky somewhere safe and protected."

"I am not running away and hiding!" Ally's chin lifted into a stubborn angle and her green eyes flashed with determination.

"That maniac is out there. He's hurt and he's angry and he will try again. I'd stake my life on it." Jim struggled to keep his voice under control. Worry and frustration warred inside him.

"That's exactly what I'm counting on," Ally replied calmly. She changed tack, speaking softly, persuasively. "Look Jim, I've had a lot of time to think, lying here. Running away won't solve anything. He'll find us and when he does, we may not be prepared for it. You've seen High Noon, haven't you? I've seen it a dozen times. It's my dad's favourite movie. Gary Cooper doesn't run. It looks like he is a hero for staying, but he simply can't run because he knows Frank Miller and his boys are going to come after him and overtake him out in the middle of nowhere. He'll have no chance in the open. His only hope is to stay in town and make a stand on his own terms. Don't you understand?"

"I guess I do," Jim admitted reluctantly, "but I am so afraid of losing you and Nicholas."

"If we do this right, you won't lose either of us. You see, I have a plan. Donna and I agree that it is the only way."

Monday 26 September

When Ally was released the next morning, her stomach was a mass of butterflies. Stepping out of the safety of the hospital was hard. She knew that Julian could be watching her every step. An open expanse of patchy lawn, bravely growing through pure white sand made up most of the hospital grounds. Here and there a low growing banksia stood hunched over under the weight of its orange flower brushes. Rainbow Lorikeets hung upside down to draw nectar from the tiny flowers that made up the brushes. They chattered noisily to each other. Occasionally the volume increased to an ear-splitting screeching, then all the birds would take off at the same time to fly around, releasing some of the sugar energy they had absorbed. Beyond the hospital gates, the ocean could be seen in the distance as an unending blue line on the horizon.

The 4WD was parked in the patient pick up zone. Ally was glad they didn't have far to go in the open. She still felt weak and lightheaded and her feet tingled with fear as she walked to the truck beside Jim. She could feel eyes boring into her back, and she had to force herself not to run back inside. Nicky sat on Jim's hip with now accustomed ease, laughing excitedly at the sight of the birds.

Ally slipped her hand into Jim's as they walked. Their steps matched perfectly. They were becoming a team. Despite the danger, she couldn't wait to be alone with the two men in her life again. The bulky dressing on her neck had been replaced by a smaller bandage, and although the wound still smarted occasionally when she moved, it was not as painful as it had been.

It was beautiful to be up high in the pickup which felt like a protector in its own right and she looked around at the bright world she had almost left in the darkness of the Oceanarium. Jim checked their suite before she and Nicky entered. It was becoming a routine. The afternoon sunshine streamed into the rooms and outside, the sea glowed a deep sparkling sapphire under a perfectly blue sky accented by fluffy white clouds that were suspended above, moving slowly westward. Jim tried to talk Ally into resting, but she couldn't bear to. After lying in a hospital bed for two days, she was as restless as Nicholas who was using the hotel sofa as a trampoline.

"I'd love a walk on the beach," she sighed.

"We really should stay here," Jim argued. "I can protect you here. If we go outside, anything could happen."

"Please Jim, there will be plenty of people on the beach and we won't stay long, I promise."

"Mama, beach!" Nicky added his voice to the conversation.

"That's it. I can't for the life of me resist the both of you."

"Great, I'll get dressed." Ally found a floaty sundress in her closet and topped it with a cotton sweater for warmth. When she back into the lounge, she found Jim putting Nicky's shoes on. The little boy lay quietly staring into Jim's face and listening to his gentle voice. She tiptoed up to them and put her hand on Jim's shoulder. "He never stays that still for me. What's your secret?"

Jim turned slightly and with one fluid movement pulled Ally into his lap. Brushing her shiny hair off her face, he leaned forward and whispered against her lips, "It's my considerable charm and charisma."

"I need convincing," Ally murmured as their lips met and clung.

Reality intruded in the form of a small boy who pushed in between them and insisted, "Beach!"

"That's a new word, you know," Ally smiled.

"We've been practising," Jim said, ruffling Nicky's hair. "Let's go then."

The Oceania was surrounded by lush tropical gardens. Palms and ferns mingled with colourful hibiscus in tones of orange, pink and red and foliage plants that Ally had only seen as houseplants grew to great sizes. Nicholas walked slowly, holding both Ally and Jim's hands down the winding path that held a surprise at every corner. A rock pool with a fountain, then a cascade into a lily pond full of goldfish kept the little boy entranced and comfortable garden benches nestled in the greenery. The path progressed into a narrow set of stairs that led down to the beach where fine white sand stretched to the rippling waves at the foreshore. Here and there a beach umbrella flowered and people lay on huge multicoloured towels soaking up the last warm rays of the sun, oblivious to everything around them.

"Let's just sit here for a while," Ally suggested finding a relatively empty stretch of sand and sinking down into its billowy warmth. Nicky plopped down beside her and immediately began running the sand through his chubby fingers.

For a while they just sat, watching the play of the sunlight on the breaking waves. Ally closed her eyes and listened to the sounds of the sea crashing into the land, mingled with the excited voices of children playing at the water's edge and the murmur of the sea breeze against her ears. It was a timeless sound, a sound of peace and happiness and carefree holidays, not of cold-eyed assassins and violent battles and blood.

With a start, Ally opened her eyes. Why did she have to have a flashback now? Tranquillity shattered like a million droplets of water soaking into the sound. Determinedly shaking off the demons, she stood up and tugged at Jim's hand. She smiled with all the reassurance she could muster at his worried frown and after a tussle with Nicky over leaving his sand pit, they walked down to the water's edge, shoes in hand.

At first, the tiny waves curling over their feet were freezing, but soon turned warm as the air grew cooler. They walked for a long time. At first, Nicky toddled between them, then on his own, falling frequently and screaming with delight, adding his happy voice to those of the other children on the beach. When he grew tired, Jim carried him on his shoulders and they kept a steady pace until the beach ended in a jumble of rocks.

They felt as though they were walking away from the danger that lurked close by, but the rocks were a reminder that they could not walk forever. As the sun began to lose intensity and sink low in the sky and the clouds blushed pink and apricot, the sea turned a soft clear green. Ally breathed deeply, bracing herself for the return, the vigil in the hotel room where the trap had been set. She paused for a second to absorb the beauty of the ocean in front of her. Jim and Nicky were a few steps away.

The sound of the waves crashing onto the rocks masked the sound of the runner until it was too late. Ally turned as the crunch of footsteps sounded right behind her. He had not waited. Julian Roche was bearing down on her like a footballer. Even as she drew breath to scream, her tackled her and drove her into the foaming water.

Waist deep, using his superior strength, he pushed her face down into the water. The sheer fabric of her dress swirled across her mouth like seaweed. Ally struggled in vain, her lungs burning with lack of oxygen.

The rock-strewn, sandy bottom rushed towards her and she felt her cheek scrape across it. Suddenly the vice like grip loosened. Ally twisted and used her hands to push off the bottom and swim to the surface.

Air entered her lungs with a painful rush. Panting, she rubbed sand and salt from her eyes to see Jim and the kidnapper a few metres away, locked in a fierce battle.

It was a clumsy, vicious fight, so unlike the choreographed masterpieces of cinema. Buffeted by the waves, the two men held onto each other as each tried to land a punch.

Ally stood deep in the water and scanned the beach for Nicholas. Finally, she spotted him, held safely by an elderly couple far up on the dry sand.

An explosive curse from Jim drew her eyes back to the fight. Julian had pulled his knife and was jabbing it at him. Already his shirt was cut open and a crimson stain soaked the fabric and spread into the water. Ally waited for the next incoming wave and followed it towards them. Julian's back was towards her, giving her the advantage this time. Using the force of the wave, she slammed into his back as hard as she could, knocking him off balance. As he fell, he looked back at her and she saw a hatred so intense blazing out of his pale eyes that she flinched. The scratches from the shell ran across his face in livid welts. The next wave covered him and he was gone.

Jim breathed a huge sigh of relief, "Thanks partner," he grinned at Ally as she waded through the water towards him. She was as ethereal as a mermaid with her streaming wet hair and dress that clung to her like a second, silky skin. She was the most beautiful woman he had ever seen and the bravest.

"We do make a great team, don't we?" she replied with a happy laugh as a wave nudged her closer.

Her green eyes sparkled as she reached her hand out. Jim touched her fingertips as the happiness fled from her face, chased by a look of puzzlement, then fear and she was sucked under the water.

"Ally!" Jim shouted above the noise of the breakers, but there would be no answer.

Ally felt herself being towed under the water by an incredibly strong force. Her ankle was held fast in an iron grip and it took all her strength to keep her head from bouncing along the rocks, millimetres below her face. She shielded herself with her arms and arched her back to try and reach the surface but it was a futile effort.

Bubbles of fear escaped her lungs and with it her hold on life started to slip. Then the frantic dash over the bottom was over. Her ankle was free. She struggled to the surface for air, but a hand pushed her head under again at the last second and she gulped sea water instead. Terror made her thrash about uselessly and with it she lost precious energy. Suddenly, she could breathe again as she was lifted through the air and deposited on something very hard and rough. Coughing and retching, she looked up through her tangled hair. She was in some sort of rock pool with high walls and slippery green rocks on every side.

Julian Roche leant above her, smiling. His eyes were so pale now, paler than the sky behind him. They looked almost as white as his hair and were filled with a maniacal enjoyment.

"Why?" she rasped. "Why?"

"I need to see you die," he grunted, his cultured accent dissolving into a growl. "You will thwart me no more."

"Please," she begged, beyond pride. "We both know you can do it, but please, don't." Even as she spoke, she knew it was a waste of her breath. He was a man possessed by pure evil, with no humanity left.

Ally gathered her last shreds of courage. If this was it, then she wouldn't give him the satisfaction of witnessing her fear, she would deny him victory.

"I'll die," she said slowly, calmly, "but I'll remember you."

Julian scowled, clearly not expecting her words, then laughed harshly. "See you in hell." With that, he pushed her under again.

Jim lurched to the spot where Ally had vanished and plunged his hands into the churning water. Nothing.

He dived under the next wave, but the bubbling water and churning sand made visibility impossible. Breaking the surface, he looked around frantically, but there was no sign of her. People on the beach were gathering, one man was scanning the waves with a pair of binoculars.

Someone had alerted the lifeguards who had been patrolling further along the beach between the flags. Four well-built young people ran along the beach in practiced strides, carrying boards, then plunged headlong into the waves on either side of Jim. They quickly paddled into deeper water.

"There's a dangerous rip here," one of them warned Jim as he sped by. "You'd better get back to the shore."

Jim nodded. He pushed the wet hair off his face. He was certain that it hadn't been a rip that had taken Ally. It was Julian Roche. Their relief had been premature. That crazed animal had taken Ally from him and could even now be killing her while he stood helpless in the shallows not knowing where to look.

Ally held her breath for as long as she could, her chest heaving with nothing to breathe until finally her mouth opened of its own volition and the bitter brine flooded her lungs. She fought violently as it happened, it was the most terrifying thing she had ever felt. Then a strange apathy invaded her. Blackness descended. She felt herself being removed from her struggling form and being drawn forward and up, towards a bright light in the sky.

It's just like the movies, she thought inanely. Maybe they were right about alien landings too. And then she flew into the light which faded, replaced by a thousand shades of green. She was walking through a park of rolling, manicured lawns that stretched as far as the eye could see. Here and there a giant oak tree spread its branches in a wide circle and banks of exquisite crimson, violet and pink rhododendrons bordered the winding path she walked along. Actually, walking seemed too mundane a word for the feeling of floating a hair's breadth above the ground. She walked for a long time, or it could have been a second.

Luke stood waiting for her in the middle of the path, arms outstretched. He looked nothing like the last time she saw him. His face shone with life and vitality. He was smiling, a great, beaming smile.

"Luke!" she cried as she ran to him. "I've missed you so much."

"My darling, so have I." They touched, and it was like clouds touching. Soft, electric, unreal.

He held her at arm's length. "You are more beautiful than ever, my darling."

His golden hair caught the light surrounding them and shone like gold. Age had not touched him, he looked young and sweet. His eyes glowed with indescribable kindness. A year had changed her so much. She felt much older than him.

"I'm so happy to be here with you," she told him. "You should see Nicholas. He is so big now and handsome. He looks just like you." She faltered. The mention of Nicky made her aware of an invisible band which was holding her rooted to the spot. She was tethered and couldn't move forward. She thought of Jim, afraid for her and the band grew wider.

Luke nodded sadly, "You can't come with me yet."

"But I want to," she pleaded, and at that moment she felt as if nothing in the world could change that.

"I know, my darling. But your time has not come yet. You have a lifetime of love to look forward to. You must raise our son to be a good man. You must love our grandchildren and when they grow up tell them how much I love them too. You must live for both of us."

"No, no!" she shook her head crying. "You can't leave me again. I can't bear it!"

"Ally," he spoke her name softly, like a raindrop falling on water, "I've been waiting for you to come. To help you back. But now I have to go forward. I have to see what's out there," he swept his arm in an arc that encompassed the trees, the hills, the light. "And you have to go back. Be happy. That man down there loves you, and...I shouldn't be telling you this, but Nicholas won't be an only child for long." He smiled and the depths of his generosity were staggering.

"Oh Luke," she fought back tears, tears that seemed to be washing away the park, the trees, the path. Finally, only Luke himself remained and then only the echo of his voice.

"Be happy, my darling."

Jim spun around. The assassin had to come ashore somewhere. It had to be on the rocks, that was the only cover on the wide beach. Even as he focused through the spray, he saw a figure straightening and scrambling away, keeping low.

It was Roche. Damn, of all the times to let his guard down and not bring his weapon. Heedless of the danger, Jim waded for the rocks, fighting strong waves every step of the way. The more logical course of action would have been to come ashore and climb down but he thought he saw something pale in the far rocks uncovered by each receding wave.

It was Ally. She lay half in and half out of the water like a sleeping mermaid with one arm flung up over her head. Her eyes were shut and her face was wet, from tears or water or both.

Jim turned back to the beach and yelled for help as loudly as his lungs would allow. Not waiting to see if he had been heard, he heaved himself over the rocks and knelt before her on the still warm surface.

Her body was icy cold. A bluish tinge inked her lips and eyelids. She wasn't breathing.

"Oh God, no," he whispered. "Don't take her away from me now. It took me a lifetime to find her." He pressed his fingertips to her throat. A faint, thready pulse beat there. She was still alive.

Moving quickly, he rolled her onto her side and thanking God for all the first aid courses he had ever taken, he checked her mouth for obstructions, then rolled her back and began CPR.

Her chest rose and fell several times before the lifesavers surrounded him. One of them tried to push him away, but he flicked the younger man out of the way as if he were a troublesome insect. Recognising his expertise, the lifesaver monitored Ally's pulse.

Through his mouth, Jim felt a slight shudder in her body, then she gasped a painful, harsh breath and coughed. Water erupted from her lungs.

The lifesavers took over then, pulling her over into the recovery position as the water drained. Ally felt herself retching over and over again. Luke was gone. No white lights, no peaceful calmness. She sobbed with the loss. But she could remember him now as he lived and as he was now. She took a deep, cleansing breath. Something else was gone. The guilt. She didn't feel guilty any more, for being the one who lived. Luke had set her free. He had let her see beyond his lifeless body. And, whatever was out there beyond life, he was eager to reach it.

Someone was wrapping a rough towel around her shoulders. Muscular men and women in red and yellow swimsuits stood around her. She lay on a stretcher, fully clothed and dripping wet. The sun had set, leaving the sky awash with pinks and mauves.

Knowing he would be there, she turned around. Jim stood beside her, arms hanging limply at his sides. Tears rolled freely down his cheeks. Ally half rose and he came to her, enfolding her in arms as strong as steel and holding her fast as if he would never let her go. Luke was right. She still had a life to live and love to give as the song said. Thank you for this, she silently thanked Luke. She felt pure joy and a will to survive such as she had never experienced before.

Jim knew that something had changed when she looked at him. Something in her eyes, some veil of sorrow that had always been there was gone. And somehow, without knowing why, he knew that the wall between them had dissolved into some sort of cosmic dust to join the universe.

Before anyone could stop her, Ally had climbed off the stretcher. Her legs were a bit wobbly but held up well. She shivered in the evening breeze.

The lifesavers were concerned. "You should be in hospital. You need to be monitored for at least 24 hours."

"And miss the last day of my vacation? I don't think so. I feel fine and Jim will look after me, as long as I can keep this towel. Thanks for saving me."

"Don't thank us, your husband did all the work. He found you. We were still searching the surf."

Ally smiled and didn't correct them, merely took his hand, squared her shoulder blades and walked off the rocks towards Nicholas.

"Jim?"

"Mm."

"Remind me to trust your instincts next time. If you don't think we should go walking, we won't."

"Agreed."

They shared the elevator to their room with an attractive young woman carrying a sleeping baby. After exchanging a few wry words about how relaxing holidays with children were, the woman got off on the floor below theirs and they continued to their suite. Nicky was asleep before they even reached the door.

Ally sighed, tomorrow she would see a doctor and get a full check-up. She had a quick shower, feeling every one of the cuts on her body, then dressed in jeans and a loose t shirt. She felt the need to be prepared for anything.

Jim found a first aid kit and bathed the scrapes on her forearms and face before changing the dressing on her neck. He seemed completely unaware of the blood-soaked mess his own shirt had become. Only after she insisted, did he take it off, revealing a jagged scratch across his lower chest. If the sea had not spoiled his aim, Julian may have killed him.

"You may need stitches," she said examining the wound.

"It's only a scratch," Jim protested as she approached him with the antiseptic.

"You're scared!" Ally was amazed.

"No, I'm not." Nevertheless, he leaned away from her hand slightly. The muscles under his skin rippled as she dabbed at the cut with a cotton ball. Her invincible hero had a tiny flaw. It made her love him even more.

"We make a good couple, don't we? The casualties of war."

"The walking wounded, do you mean? I'd say we're survivors. We'll need to be, soon. Put that disgusting stuff down. There's only so much disinfecting I can handle. Need to have a shower anyway!"

Ally laughed and walked into the kitchen to make a cup of tea. Sometime later, as they were curled up together on the sofa, Ally looked up at him seriously, "You know what they say, don't you?"

"No, what do they say?"

"That if you save someone's life, you are responsible for them for ever."

"I would be honoured," he smiled.

"It may not be an easy task. With him on the loose," she mused.

"I can handle it," he said with quiet assurance.

"Talking of handling things... don't you think it's about time I learnt how to use that gun of yours?"

"I thought you didn't like guns."

"I like being completely helpless while someone does their damnedest to kill me even less. I guess I'm just sick of being the victim."

Jim nodded grimly, remembering the sight of her lifeless body in the rock pool. If anyone had a right to defend herself, it was Ally. He pulled the .45 out of its holster and handed it to her. She cradled it in both hands, feeling the comforting heaviness. The metal wasn't black as she first thought, but had a deep, deep blue tinge to it and a slightly oily sheen. The potential power of the weapon seemed to emanate from it, even as it lay across her palms.

"It's very simple really, which is why so many lowlifes can work it out. Barrel, keep the business end pointed away from yourself, down usually. Keep your arms close to your body, not stretched out too far. Rest the butt on your left palm like this and hold it with your right. Safety on and off. Trigger, rest your forefinger on it very lightly until you need to shoot, then squeeze it until it goes bang. This button is the mag release. You won't need it because there are sixteen bullets ready to go. If the first shot doesn't connect, try again. Aim for the body, don't try anything tricky like an arm shot because this man is a proven killer. Just wounding him won't stop him. And don't forget, this thing kicks like a mule."

The matter-of-fact way he said it spoke of years of experience. Ally wondered if he was even aware of how much he was giving away about his past. If she had not stopped him the other night, he would have confided in her, trusted her enough to share that painful chapter with her. She knew now that they were meant to be together forever, if they could just survive the next encounter with Julian Roche.

Jim showed her how to stand and take aim. His arms encircled her as he curved her fingers under his on the gun. The heady heat of his body barely touching her back sent waves of longing through her until she just wanted to forget all the violence yet to come and concentrate on their love. But she couldn't. Not yet.

"That is enough to get you out of trouble," Jim continued, unaware of her thoughts. She slid the gun back into its holster. He was so afraid for her that he felt sick, but he tried not to show it. She needed his strength now. Not his fears.

He had fought with Roche twice now, and knew that in a fair fight, he could win. But the man was a killer, a professional hitman. Fighting fair was not on his agenda. The way he attacked Ally though, first at the Oceanarium, then in the water today, was not the way a professional would act. He was letting his emotions control him and that gave Jim the advantage. It made the killer dangerous and unpredictable but Roche would not be satisfied with a long-distance rifle shot. He would come in close for the kill. Jim was sure of it. And this time he would be ready.

Summoning up a smile, Jim pulled Ally close and held her tightly.

The evening dragged on. Seconds ticked by, endlessly rolling into minutes, then hours as the flickering television screen did nothing to dispel the tension surrounding them as they sat entwined on the sofa.

"He's near, I can feel him."

Jim agreed. "There's nothing like a near death experience to hone the senses. Especially the sense of self preservation. What was it like?"

"My near-death experience?"

He nodded.

"I really don't know. I didn't get past the front door as it were. For a while there, I was willing to give up everything to find out. But then I remembered Nicholas, and I remembered you." Ally stroked his beard roughened face. "I wasn't ready to let the two of you go." She looked up into his grey eyes until Jim thought she could see through his lies. Could she forgive him? She would be so hurt. At this instant, he couldn't risk it. So, he said nothing.

"The next few hours are going to be rough, aren't they?" she asked.

"He may not even come. I miscalculated badly this afternoon. The only thing we do know is that he is unpredictable."

"You should have seen the look in his eyes, Jim. He was like a man driven, obsessed. He can't stop, even if he wanted to."

"Well, we'd better get some sleep then, so we can tackle him head on as soon as he makes his move."

CHAPTER EIGHT

Julian Roche stood silently in the grounds of the Oceania, looking up at her window. There were hundreds of windows, but he knew which one was Alexandria Reed's. Even if he had not counted the floors, he would still have known. He had worked for many years, first in Europe then in Australia. Always completely professional, his terminations had always been clean, untraceable. Since his first encounter with Conrad, and more importantly Reed, his impassivity had deserted him. Maybe it was the time spent with the defenceless infant that had clouded his judgement. He had never had the desire to procreate, even to be in the presence of children. Children were something to be avoided. They were loud and demanding and smelled funny.

But from the moment he saw the two imbeciles with the child, he had felt an overwhelming protective urge towards the small boy. He could not explain it. It was a feeling too strong, yet too tenuous to pin down. He had killed the two lackeys without a second thought, but he had picked the infant up tenderly, marvelling at its soft skin and gently rounded limbs. He had looked into those wide blue eyes, full of innocence and trust and a part of him had changed forever.

At that moment, he had known that he could not give the boy to the old man for his evil purpose, but would keep him for himself. It would be an easy enough task to make an addition to his passport and take him out of the country as soon as the furore had died down.

He had planned to drive to Brisbane where it would be easy to disappear, but the small boy had begun crying, unable to travel any more. Julian had stopped for the child's sake. It was a mistake, for she found him easily. She had bested him. She and that boyfriend of hers. She had humiliated him and taken the child that he wanted more than anything.

When his client had cancelled the contract due to his failure, he had not objected. This assignment had become very personal. He had bought a blade. He had been so close. And still she defeated him. But in the ocean this afternoon he had won. Or so he thought. His triumph had been short lived. Conrad had saved her, brought her back from the dead, because that was where he had left her. With the dead.

It was time to stop being sentimental. This time there would be no prolonged goodbyes, no job satisfaction. He would simply terminate her, and Conrad.

The flickering light in her room went out. The whole floor was in darkness. Julian laughed. Sleep, you innocent fools, sleep. It was the midnight hour. The hour of the hunter.

Slowly, he sauntered across the lawn and began the long climb to his objective. It won't be long now, Mrs Reed, he thought.

His muscles strained against his black shirt as he pulled himself up and over the balcony belonging to her room. All was quiet. Easing his gun from its holster, he carefully screwed in the silencer, then quietly prised the lock on the glass sliding door and crept into what looked like a living room. A quick sweep with his flashlight confirmed his first impression. The room was empty. Cushions on the sofa still bore the imprints of two bodies that had sat close. His mouth drew into a sneer of distaste. They made him sick. These love birds. The sooner they were dead, the happier he would be.

The first bedroom he found was empty too. The window was open and the filmy curtains swayed in the warm breeze. Crouching as he crept into the second bedroom, he had to stifle a croak of satisfaction that rose in his throat at the sight of the two people in the huge bed in the centre of the room. Next to the bed stood a cot, he could see it in the dim glow coming from the window. He did not dare use his flashlight but his eyes were accustomed to the darkness now.

For the briefest moment, he considered just taking the boy and leaving, without the blood of its mother on his hands. But the feeling disappeared as quickly as it had formed. He couldn't let her live. She was a determined and resourceful woman. She would never rest until she found them. It was better to start afresh, with no ties to the past. Julian turned his attention back to the bed.

One of the sleeping forms was snoring softly, obviously the man. He would be the first to go. In rapid succession, the assassin fired two bullets into each form.

The snoring continued. Julian frowned. The hairs on the back of his neck stood up. His instincts had been dulled by his need for revenge, his need for the child. Now he realised that something was very wrong.

He ripped the soft duvet from the bed. As he had suspected, there were no bodies there, only pillows lined up on either side of a phone that continued to snore, mocking him. Slowly, he crouched, like an animal presenting the smallest possible target, listening. Somewhere in the shadows was a sound so slight that most would not have heard it. The sound of quiet breathing, a heartbeat. It was coming from behind him, near the doorway.

It was a trap. Was Conrad alone? In the darkness he couldn't be sure of his aim. Jim waited. The assassin crouched, facing him in the darkness. The man was expecting him to switch the light on. So, he didn't. He could feel the other man's, barely reined in patience, slipping. A little wait would drive him crazy. It might give Jim the edge.

Suddenly, Roche sprang towards him, firing. The bullets were uncomfortably close, skimming past his shoulder and Jim fired at the flashes in the darkness. But his target was moving too quickly, across the room, past him and into the lounge. That is when the light did come on, showing the half dozen police, weapons drawn.

Without hesitation, Julian fired into their midst and dove onto the balcony. Face to face with Alexandria Reed. It was obvious she had not expected him to run the gauntlet quite so easily. She had been hiding here waiting for him to be killed. Well, she would be the one killed. Right here, under a starry midnight sky. Julian loved the way her green eyes widened with shock and fear as she realised who had appeared beside her.

"This will be the last time we meet, Mrs Reed," he snarled, raising the gun to point it straight between those eyes.

Ally's mouth opened to speak, but she couldn't make a sound. Her throat had tightened so much. She saw the small black opening in the gun barrel pointed right at her and she froze in terror.

"Stop right there!" Jim's voice sounded from inside the room.

In response, Julian lunged at Ally and spun her around so she shielded him from the other man. She felt the cold metal of the gun pressed against the small of her back. Still, she couldn't move. The feel of Julian Roche's hands on her, the sweet, sandalwood scent he wore combined to form the smell of death. She felt so numb and cold, like she was drowning again and just had to let go. One thought kept her from collapsing. She was not alone this time. Ally managed to look at Jim, who had stepped into the doorway. His gun was drawn, but he had lost that calm confidence she so envied. He was as afraid as she was. He was afraid for her, in a hopeless situation.

The sight of his vulnerability gave her strength. She could not just stand there and expect him to save her. The only way out was if they worked as a team.

Slowly, the feeling returned to her body and she began to think again.

"Just drop your gun like a good little guard dog," Julian smirked, "and tell the others to do the same or your lady friend is history."

Jim felt sick. Ally's face blurred before him. He was in a restaurant. The smell of garlic was overpowering. The man in front of him gave one look as if to say, see, you can't even trust your friends. Then the young woman was lying there, dead. The hostage became Ally lying in the rockpool, was it only this afternoon?

"Drop it, Conrad."

He jolted back into the present and placed his .45 at his feet.

"Come on out and lock that door behind you. Three's company, Sixteen's too much of a party for me. Now drop the key over the edge."

Jim complied, furious with himself for not foreseeing this possibility. He should have made sure Ally was safely away from this place. Now it was just the three of them with the ocean crashing somewhere in the darkness. Jim could not keep the guilt from his eyes as he looked at Ally clearly for the first time. What he saw made him frown in confusion. She was smiling. One eyebrow raised in that delightful way she had. Then she looked down. He followed her eyes. She was holding the same razor-sharp shell that had saved her life at the Oceanarium.

"You know, Jules," she said softly, not bothering to keep the confident amusement out of her voice, "you really should give up now while you still have a chance."

Roche opened his mouth to laugh, but it changed to a grunt as she plunged the shell into his black trousered thigh and used all her strength to break free from his grasp and drop to the ground. Jim was on him in an instant, wrestling him to the balcony floor. She was free of him. Jim would be able to beat him more easily now, he had done it before.

Giddy with relief, she scrambled on her hands and knees until she reached the .45. Whether she could use it was another matter. With trembling hands, she undid the safety and pushed the hammer back before turning it to point at the two men. There was no way to get a clear shot. For a split second, Jim had the upper hand, his body half across Roche's before they rolled and the other man had the advantage, smashing his fists into Jim's face. Jim avoided most of the blows, but not all and blood welled at the corner of his mouth.

Frowning fiercely in concentration, Ally aimed the pistol. No, it was no use. The risk of hitting Jim by mistake was too great. She let the weapon hang heavily by her side. The sound of shouting drew her eyes reluctantly to the interior of the suite. The police officers were asking her to unlock the door. They looked a little ludicrous gesturing from behind the safety of a glass door while the two civilians they had meant to protect were fending for themselves. Ally tried to summon some anger at their ineptitude, but she couldn't. They had all underestimated the power and cunning of Julian Roche.

"I can't," she shouted back, "I don't have the key."

"Then step back, we'll break the glass."

Ally did her best but there was no room. She was pressed against the far edge of the balcony as it was, and she had no desire to come any closer to the two fighting men. She would only be in Jim's way. She shrugged at the police and turned back to where the dull sounds of blows contacting flesh and bone turned her blood cold. For the first time, she wondered if Jim could do it.

They were standing, locked together now, neither man giving an inch. Even though Jim was taller than Roche and broader at the shoulders and possibly the stronger of the two, he had one disadvantage. He was fighting a man on the verge of insanity. An insanity that kept him intensely powerful.

Jim was holding his own, but for how long? Ally looked at his exhausted, bleeding face and knew he was almost at the end of his strength. She couldn't bear it, not Jim too. She couldn't bear to lose him. Even as she watched, the two slammed into the edge of the balcony and it shook under their combined weight. Julian pushed Jim's upper body over the edge and Ally let out an involuntary scream. Roche turned with a smug grin, momentarily losing concentration and Jim used the distraction to strike his opponent one last time. Roche cursed, lunged again and before Ally's horrified vision, both men toppled over the edge.

She ran to the edge and looked over. Jim was hanging on with both hands. The other man clung to his trouser leg like a grotesque crow, his legs flailing. Ally dropped the gun and crouched down to grasp Jim's forearm through the bars of the railing, taking as much weight as she could until he was able to hook his elbow around one of the railings. She could hear the sound of glass breaking behind her.

Roche was not letting go. Ally looked past Jim to see the other man reach into his pocket and pull out the little knife.

"Don't do it!" she screamed at him. "You'll both fall!"

Julian, face flushed with the effort of holding on single handed, grinned that evil grin of his. "I know."

"I don't think he's kidding," Jim groaned, realising what was happening even though he could only see Ally's anguished expression.

Looking into his icy eyes, Ally knew the assassin was willing to die, just to take Jim with him. Without stopping to think, she picked up the gun again. She was vividly aware of each passing second, of the sound of the ocean, the smell of the salt air, the swift beating of her own heart. Just as he was raising his knife arm to strike, she aimed and a loud gunshot fired beside her ear, stunning her. She dropped the gun in shock as the police flooded onto the tiny balcony. Jim!

Her love was still there, panting with the effort, but holding on strongly, with the biggest smile she had ever seen on his face. She grasped his elbow and hung on for dear life, trying not to look at the still, misshapen body on the ground far below.

"Thanks mate," he spoke to the blue uniformed officer who was putting away his firearm hurriedly and crouching down to grasp Jim's other hand. Someone nudged Ally out of the way and took over to pull Jim back up and over the railing. The whole ordeal had taken only seconds but felt like a lifetime. She sat on the cool balcony tiles, reaction setting in. She shook and tried not to vomit. She had almost taken a life. The gun lay beside her. She felt so sorry for the young officer who had fired. He had to live with that forever. But Jim was alive and that was all that mattered. There was no other choice. Apart from looking even more like the walking wounded, Jim seemed perfectly normal and cheerful. He hugged her tightly and kissed the top of her head. "It's over. They got him. We're safe now." She looked at him numbly and nodded, still not able to stand up or even move.

Jim scooped her up and carried her inside, laying her carefully on the sofa and finding a throw to tuck around her legs. Ally just didn't know what to do next. The fear she had lived with for so long was gone, the relief was so extreme, it left her spent. Somebody moved beside her and a weight settled on her lap. She looked down numbly. It was her little boy. He was sound asleep despite the noise and lights around him. Tears streamed down her face as she realized he would be safe now.

Donna put her arm around Ally's shoulders and gave her a sisterly hug. Ally looked at her with gratitude, "Thank you so much for looking after Nicky, Donna. Thank goodness he wasn't here."

"My pleasure, he's a great little kid. Our plan to swap him for "my" baby in the lift was brilliant. Roche

226

didn't suspect a thing and walked straight into our trap."

"And straight out of it," Ally laughed.

"Yes, well, that will be all in the report. Paper work is the worst part of this job," she sighed. Ally could see that Donna felt that she was responsible. If she had been in the suite instead of babysitting, things may have turned out differently. But, being the professional she was, she said nothing.

"If he had gotten his hands on Nicky again, it would have been a disaster, I will always be in your debt." Ally reassured the other woman.

"All good. Unfortunately, this lovely suite is now a crime scene and we will have to relocate you to the floor below after your statements are completed," Donna shrugged apologetically.

Ally looked at Jim who came over immediately. "I can't wait till we can go home. This holiday has been way too much fun."

CHAPTER NINE

Tuesday 27 September

Ally unlocked her front door and slipped gratefully into the quiet interior. She looked back at Jim, carrying a wriggling Nicky. The little boy had definitely had enough of cars and travelling. Jim set him down and Ally steadied him. He struggled out of her grip and toddled happily down the hallway. Ally watched him disappear into the lounge before turning back to Jim. He seemed to be waiting. She stepped up to him and wrapped her arms around his waist. He hugged her back quietly.

Jim felt as if this moment was what he had been waiting for his entire life. Among the high fliers of the corporate world, he had met many women but none that had made him feel, beyond certainty, that they belonged together, like Ally did. He needed her in his life forever, not just for a few days. A lifetime would not be enough.

As he stood holding her, he knew he could no longer keep any secrets from her.

"Ally," he said to the top of her head, "I need to tell you something about myself and I don't think you are going to like it. You may never want to see me again."

Ally pulled away from him slightly and looked up at him with a puzzled frown. Jim saw the trust in her clear green eyes. This was going to be even more difficult than he had imagined. A question formed on her lips. Then she looked past him through the open doorway at the brilliant sunshine outside.

Jim saw her eyes narrow, then grow wide with shock and fear. He followed her gaze. There, like a golden maned lion, stood Max Reed. Jim felt Ally press closer to him as if seeking protection. Damn, he thought, of all the lousy timing.

"Alexandria." Max nodded a greeting. "Conrad, a job well done. You really earned your money this time." His deep baritone rumbled like a death knell to Jim's relationship with Ally.

He felt Ally shrinking away from him. "You know this man?" she asked with pained disbelief. How could she have been so wrong about someone? How could she have let herself fall in love with him? How could she have let him into her son's life?

Jim's heart tore as he looked at the pain his betrayal had brought to Ally. It was what he had been afraid of all along. He wanted to deny it, to tell her what she wanted to hear, but he couldn't. She needed the truth from him above all else right now. She may never be able to trust him again, or even want to see him, but he would never lie to her again.

"Yes," Jim admitted. "That is what I had to tell you. What I've been trying to tell you."

"You set me up!" she accused bitterly. "You were part of this kidnapping right from the start."

"No, I was hired to protect you."

Ally shook her head. "He's a murderer Jim."

"What?" Max thundered. He had been listening to this exchange for long enough and was not a patient man.

"You had my husband murdered and you kidnapped my son. Oh my God." Ally backed away from them. "It's my turn, isn't it?"

"Ally, you're wrong," Jim insisted, reaching out to her. She flinched away.

"Shut up Conrad. She's my sister-in-law, even though she's an idiot." Max turned his intense blue gaze on her. "Don't you realize that you and little Nicholas are my family? I would never do anything to harm you."

He seemed so sincere. Ally didn't know what to think. For so long, she had believed Luke. That Max was the enemy. But now she realized that they could both have been wrong.

"Luke said you blamed him for the death of your family," Ally insisted.

"Luke blamed himself. At first, I was so wrapped up in my own grief to see what was happening. When I tried to tell him it was an accident, he had already discharged himself from the hospital and disappeared. I thought, in time, we would reconnect. I never thought Luke's time would run out." Sorrow etched deep into Max's features.

"If you didn't kill him, then who did?" Ally questioned, faltering in her conviction.

"I don't know. It might have been an accident. But I couldn't be sure. I have made enemies along the way. You and Nicholas were the next likely targets, which is why I hired Conrad to keep an eye on you."

"Why?"

"Nicholas is my heir," Max replied as if that explained everything.

Ally turned to Jim sadly, "So everything you told me was a lie."

"No! Luke was my friend. We had lost touch, but that is why I agreed to help Max. To protect my friend's family." Jim looked at her intently. His eyes told her that he didn't lie about loving her either.

She stared back bleakly, as if she had lost her best friend. "I need to think about all of this," she said. "I would like the both of you to leave. Now."

"You may still be in danger," Max warned.

"I will be until you've left," she retorted.

"Call me if you need anything," Max offered as he walked towards the sunshine outside. Ally felt a pang of grief as the sunlight glinted off his golden mane. He looked like Luke. There was no doubt they were brothers. She watched him walk away from her and for a moment wanted to call him back. He had already lost so much. The moment passed. Jim paused and if he was going to say something, then turned on his heel and followed.

"Goodbye." Ally said firmly as she began to close the door. Making up his mind, Jim turned and shot out a hand that stopped the door in mid swing.

"Take this." He urged, pressing a small black plastic box into her hand and closing her slim fingers around it with his own. Ally froze at the contact. Jim noticed. "It's an emergency beeper."

"I won't need it." She said, putting it into her pocket nevertheless.

"I'm so sorry." He said sombrely as she closed the door on him.

CHAPTER TEN

Nicky was playing happily in the kitchen, oblivious to the turmoil his mother was feeling. He looked up as she came in, then went back to opening the drawers she had designated for his toys. Finding his familiar treasures, he made little grunts of satisfaction.

"Oh, my little darling," she smiled through unshed tears as she knelt down beside him, dropping her bag to the ground. When Luke had died, she had not allowed herself to be consumed by grief, for the sake of her baby, and she wasn't about to start now. Despite his lies and betrayal, Jim had reunited her with Nicky and she couldn't find it in her heart to hate him. Who was she trying to kid? She loved him. Nothing could change that. When she loved someone, it was unconditional.

He had tried to tell her something a few times. She had assumed it was about his past as a hostage negotiator, but now she knew he had been about to tell her about his involvement with Max Reed. It was her own fault that she had not heard him out, but she had had other things on her mind. Her hand involuntarily touched her stomach, where even now perhaps a new life grew, a life that came from their love.

Soon she would call him, but not yet. She was still angry at being manipulated both by him and Max.

Her brother-in-law was an enigma. She had feared him from afar for so long that he had grown larger than life in her imagination. Curiously, after meeting him, he hadn't diminished. He wore the mantle of power well. Except for their looks, he and Luke seemed completely different. Max didn't have any of Luke's vulnerability. But could she believe him? Did he have a deadly adversary who was attacking him through his family? It hardly seemed possible. What could he have done to cause someone to hate him so much? Could she suspend her past certainty of Max's guilt? Ally was so deep in thought that she didn't hear the footsteps behind her until a familiar voice spoke.

"Ah, Ally, my dear, you are back! And the little man of the house too!" chuckled Charlie's familiar voice behind her.

"Yes Charlie, he's home safe." Ally smiled at her neighbour happily. "I'm so sorry I didn't ring you with the news, haven't even rung Mum and Dad yet, but we're home safely now."

Charlie stooped down to Nicky who promptly climbed onto his lap. He rose slowly, still cuddling Nicky who had wrapped his arms around Charlie's neck. He was the only grandfather her son had ever known. Charlie hugged him back.

"Thank goodness for that. I was so worried. I hope you don't mind me coming in like this. I used the spare key. Thought I'd water your plants."

"Thank you so much Charlie. You are such a good friend to us."

Charlie smiled benignly. What a naïve and stupid woman she was.

Ally noticed something odd about his expression. "Are you feeling ok..." her voice trailed off uncertainly and she blinked, twice. Her friendly neighbour, still holding Nicky with one arm, pointed an evil looking black revolver at her.

"What," she asked numbly, "are you doing Charlie?"

"I'm making sure no brat is going to carry on the Reed line. Maxwell's own family is dead. A perfect little accident, even if I say so myself. He is the last. I want him to suffer as I have suffered all these years." He grinned then, an ugly, crooked grin that made Ally's skin crawl. Max was right after all. There was someone who hated him enough to wipe out his entire family, including tiny, innocent Nicky. But, Charlie? He was her friend, her shoulder to cry on when life became overwhelming. All the times he had consoled her after Luke's death... She just couldn't believe it was Charlie. And now he was about to pull the trigger and end it all. You may not be out of danger yet, she remembered Jim saying. Jim! He could still help, if only there was time.

Keep him talking, she thought. Her hand inched into her pocket and pressed the beeper Jim had given her. "I don't understand any of this."

"You, my dear, don't really matter. You are just a nuisance to me, you and your new boyfriend. Flies in my cooking pot. All those heroics."

"Tell me why," she insisted. "Why are you doing these awful things to us?"

Charlie's eyes took on a faraway look as he began to unfold a terrible tale. "Maxwell killed my son in his damn lumber mill twenty years ago. He was only eighteen, my Andy. On holidays. He was going to be an engineer you know."

Ally nodded, not trusting herself to say anything.

"He was a good son. He was the one brilliant thing in our lives, my wife's and mine. We were poor then, but we made sure Andy had the best of everything. Andy didn't want me working overtime at the mill to pay for his education. He said I had done so much for him already. He said he would work with me, to make some extra cash. He wanted to send his mother and me on a cruise when he graduated. He always worried about us. I told him it was too dangerous, that he should just concentrate on study, but his mind was made up. I asked my boss to take him on. A young upstart, he was, just a little older than my Andy. Not worth the mud on Andy's shoes. He was jealous of how smart Andy was.

"On his first day, Maxwell assigned him to the chip compressor machine. Said he could do it, seeing he was so bright. Well, it caught Andy's arm and pulled him in. I was on the other side of the floor. It took me precious seconds to get to him. The machine crushed him bit by bit. I tried to pull him out, but it caught me too. That's how this happened." He rubbed his crippled leg with his gun. His voice grew deep with hatred. "Then that bastard turned off the machine and pulled me out. He saved me and I had to watch my son die."

"Oh no." Ally said, with her hand to her mouth in shock. He went on as if she had not spoken at all.

"He was my life, my Andy. I thought I'd go mad. My wife did. She's still in the institution. Doesn't recognise me."

"What about your daughter?"

"I have no daughter. I made her up to put you at ease. I have no one."

"Oh Charlie," Ally breathed, "I'm so sorry for your loss."

"Don't give me your useless sympathy my dear. I've waited all these years for my revenge and now I will have it. Settle old scores if you will."

"But how will hurting us settle your score? We had not even met Max until today. He doesn't know or care about us."

"You are mistaken. You are his only remaining family. I made sure of that. And family is important to him. Little Nicholas here is his heir. Don't forget, I heard every word he said to you. He wants to become part of your lives. My timing is perfect. Now I can put a stop to that. He will be as alone as I am for the rest of his life. He will live in misery forever, knowing that he has been the cause of so many deaths. My Andy, his pregnant wife, his brother's innocent little family. It's really amusing in a way. I will have paid him back with interest."

"You caused the accident that killed Katie?" it all made sense now. None of it had been by chance. And it hadn't been Luke's fault either. He had lived with all that guilt and died believing that he had been responsible, when all the time it had been this grief-twisted, evil man who had been the cause. Poor Luke. His image stabilized her thoughts. Wherever he was now, he must know the truth. He knew it wasn't her time yet. She couldn't give up now, for Nicky's sake.

She tried again. "You can't really hurt us, Charlie, we're friends."

Charlie sighed in mock regret. "It's true, despite myself, I like you. You are a very nice young lady and have been good to an old man like me. I found it difficult to hurt you. That's why I hired a "professional" who turned out to be an overemotional idiot. But his failures have strengthened my resolve. I just wish Maxwell could be here to witness the impotence of his wealth. The look in his eyes when he realizes that there is nothing, he can do, to save you."

Ally saw the fanatical gleam in his eyes, the same gleam Julian Roche had in his pale eyes while he held her under the water in the rock pool. She had survived then, and she would survive now. A growing anger fuelled her courage. This old, bitter man had no right to take away her future and her son's future just because he had lost his son in a tragic accident. Despite everything he had done, she still felt sorry for Charlie, or whatever his name was. His life had been torn apart and had destroyed the good man he had once been. But she was sure he still had goodness buried deep in his broken heart.

Feeling sympathy for him was not going to prevent him from carrying out his diabolical plans. That was up to her. She had to keep thinking. She moved infinitely closer to her little boy.

"And now you are going to kill us?" she asked in as calm a voice as she could muster.

"Not me. The fire. It's these old houses, you know. Go up like a bonfire. I've taken the precaution of sprinkling a little of your excellent furniture cleaner around. The label assures me it is flammable."

"Charlie, that's crazy. You can't just light a fire with that stuff around. We'll all die. You won't be able to get away from it fast enough. You know how much that leg of yours hurts if you move too fast. Please, Charlie, don't do this." She found she was babbling. She was so afraid of fire. It destroyed so quickly, so thoroughly. If you survived, the pain and disfigurement lasted for life. She couldn't let that happen to her baby boy. She had to get him away from Charlie.

He clicked his tongue reproachfully. "Shame on you Ally. You'll have me believing you care for me even now. You would be happy to see me dead after what I did to your loving husband. Not to mention what I am about to do to your child. Don't try and play me for a fool. I'm not. I can see through your ploy. You won't stop me with your pretty words and kind smiles. I have to do this for my Andy. Andy should have been the one with the family now, not you."

"Surely if Andy was the boy, you say he was, he wouldn't want you to do this to us. He would want you to find some peace and remember him the way he was."

"Shut up!"

Ally stopped. She saw she had said too much. She had made the old man angry. He had turned an alarming dark red and shook with rage. "Shut up I tell you. You did not know Andy. You don't know what he would have wanted. You are a devious woman and I will not listen to your lies about my son anymore. No more talking. I have had enough of you."

Ally knew her time was almost up.

Charlie tucked the gun into his belt and took out a lighter. He glared at her with hatred. She wasn't sure if he even recognized her any more. As he fumbled with it one handed, Ally lunged for Nicky, tore him out of Charlie's grip and scooped him up, then turned and ran down the hallway. Charlie's roar of anger followed. A faint but unmistakable crackling sound told her the fire was lit.

The front door was dead locked. Her keys were in her bag, lying on the kitchen floor, so was her phone. She looked back. Charlie was standing there, despite the flames, waiting. She swung into the front bedroom whose windows opened onto the veranda. As she slammed the door behind them, a metallic sound reached her ears. She was just in time to see a series of thick iron bars slide down the window and lock into position on a new steel window sill. An ominous darkness shrouded the room. He had thought of everything. That was why he wasn't bothering to follow her. Losing hope, she tried her bedroom. It was dimmer too. Smoke was starting to billow down the hall. Nicky whimpered, knowing something was wrong.

The first bedroom was the one furthest from the fire. Ally ran back into it and slammed the door. She sat Nicky on the floor in the corner, murmuring softly to him and then dragged the blankets off the bed to wedge them against the door.

She went to Nicky and gathered his small body close to hers and prayed for Jim to hurry. She knew he would come, but would he be in time? Tendrils of smoke curled into the room. It was growing hotter too.

In minutes the room would succumb to the assault of the fire.

Ally pulled the beeper out of her pocket. The LCD display was blank.

"Oh no," she cried, shaking it in a futile attempt to make it work, then she noticed the small black switch on the side. "You idiot!" she admonished herself, sliding it to ON. Wasting no more time, she pressed the beeper. This time it did work.

Breathing a sigh of relief, she rocked Nicky back and forth, keeping his face pressed against her and crooned to him softly, even as the smoke made her voice hoarse and her eyes sting.

Darling Luke, she thought. Maybe you were wrong. Maybe it is our time to join you. But, not Nicky. Not like this. Luke didn't appear. Instead, an image of Jim, strong, calm, invincible came to mind. She imagined his arms going around her gently. She imagined his lips touching her forehead. She imagined him telling her he loved her.

"I love you too, Jim. Never doubt it," Ally realized she had spoken out loud.

Jim frowned as he continued to throw shirts and trousers haphazardly into his suitcase. The emptiness of his impersonal apartment mocked him. Ally was right when she said you only started truly living when you loved someone. And he loved Ally, and Nicholas, more than he would have even dreamed. And he had betrayed her, lied to her.

She could not forgive him. He knew that now. She had trusted him completely. The look of hurt and shock in her eyes when she had found out that he was just a worthless minion of Max Reed's had shown him that.

Everything he had said and done since the moment they met, and even before that, was a lie. A low down, worthless lie. He had taken advantage of her. You love her and that's not a lie, a voice inside his head said.

"Damn," he swore, raking his fingers savagely through his hair. "What sort of human being are you to sink to doing a job like this?"

He didn't know what he would do next. The lies, the deceptions, were over. He would take some time off. Do some travelling. Enjoy his freedom and independence. Try to forget what it felt like to have someone love him. To hear a quiet voice whisper to him in the dark. To have someone to hold next to him. To play with a child who had become so dear to him in a few short days.

He looked at the pathetic suitcase that was his life. No, he couldn't forget. Running away wouldn't help. He had to stay and fight for her love.

Feeling exhilarated at his decision, Jim upended his suitcase onto the bed, covering it with a jumble of clothes. It would be hard work, winning Ally's trust, but he had one thing in his favour. A love like theirs does not just die. He was sure of it.

Deciding to give her space though, was a good idea. She must be so angry with him at the moment. He had to stay away for now. Walking into the tiny kitchen he stared into the fridge. It was depressingly bare, and the food that was there, had long since deteriorated into something that looked like one of his high school biology experiments. Jim couldn't quite remember what it was. Cheese maybe, or takeout. Sure smelled bad now, though. He would have to go out and buy some steak. Thinking about a solitary dinner left him even more depressed. Well, there was no avoiding it tonight. Jim pulled on his jacket and turned towards the door.

A beep from his fax stopped him in his tracks. Frowning, Jim took the paper from it. His knuckles whitened as he read the copy of an old newspaper clipping that had emerged.

The piercing tones of the beeper sounded from his jacket pocket. Ally! She was calling him. She wanted to see him again. Even as his heart lifted, he looked out of the window towards her little house below.

What he saw chilled him to his core. A thick plume of grey smoke was billowing up from the back of the house.

Fire!

He flew from his room, dialling 000 as he ran for the elevators. He hit the lift button so hard with the heel of his hand that he almost cracked its plastic casing. Thankfully, it was a new building and the lift was fast and efficient. Within seconds he was riding down to the ground floor and out onto the street. The smell of the house on fire carried on the wind as he ran towards it. The house looked different. As he ran up the steps, two at a time, he realised that every window was barred. Why had he not seen them before, when he had brought Ally and Nicholas home? It was because you were stupidly happy, the voice in his head said. You stopped being their protector.

Where were they? The rear of the house was ablaze how, roaring fiercely. If she was there...he would not think of that. She had to be at the front of the house.

"Ally!" he screamed. "Ally, answer me!" He slammed his fist into the door until it shook. Taking a few steps backwards, he rushed at the door, trying to force it open. And almost broke his shoulder. It had been reinforced with something too. There was no way to get in through the front of the house and flames were licking through the windows further back. He had to think and think fast. First, he had to find out where Ally and Nicky were.

Ally prayed that death would come quickly and that Nicky would not suffer too much. They pressed closer to the floor where the air was clearer. She imagined that Jim was calling her name. The sound of his voice made her sob. She must be hallucinating from the smoke.

Then she heard loud banging at the front door. It was Jim. He had come. She didn't know how. She had only pressed the beeper a minute ago. He called her name again.

"Jim!" she yelled out between coughs, "Jim, we're in here. We can't get out."

Nicky, startled by the panic in her voice, started crying and dissolved into coughing as smoke entered his lungs. Then he began to quieten as she whispered to him, "Shh sweetheart, it's going to be OK. It's all right." No matter what happened, she would have to shield him from her own terror. That thought made her infinitesimally stronger. The need to protect her son diminished her fear. The fire crackled at the back of the house. Mocking her.

"Ally, where are you. Exactly."

"In my bedroom. Hurry Jim, I can't keep the smoke out."

"I'll get you out love. Get off the floor and onto the bed."

"What, that's crazy," but she climbed onto the bed anyway, dragging Nicholas up with her.

She heard his footsteps thumping down the stairs and the distant wail of sirens. The atmosphere was slowly thickening with acrid smoke. Paint began to blister and pop adding a sweet smell to the mix that made her gag. She pushed Nicky's face into her chest and covered him with a sheet. He had stopped crying and that scared her even more.

Suddenly there was a sound of a motor starting, faltering, starting again. The metallic whine of a chainsaw. Ally had never heard a sweeter sound. Jim was using Luke's chainsaw to cut them out. She had not had the heart to sell any of his tools.

The teeth of the saw bit into the wood beneath them and then the bar emerged in a spray of sawdust. It started slicing through the floorboards as if they were butter. Within seconds, a three-foot cut had been completed and the bar vanished, only to appear at a right angle to the first cut. Sawdust flew everywhere as the chainsaw noisily chewed the floor. Ally laughed hysterically, because she would never have to sweep it up.

A third cut completed a crude triangle and the boards fell through the hole to the ground below. Jim's sawdust enveloped head and shoulders appeared.

"Come on sleepyheads," he said. "This is no time to be lying around in bed."

"Anything you say," Ally coughed. "Nicky, sweetheart, we're going to play a little wombat game now. You're the little wombat and Mummy wombat is going to pass you into the big wombat hole to Jim wombat, Ok?"

Nicholas shook his head, "Naughty wombie."

Ally lowered him down to Jim, trying not to scrape his legs on the splintered edges. Just as she felt Jim take his weight, there was a crash behind her. Ally spun around and couldn't suppress a scream as part of the ceiling caved in on top of the bed. Flames erupted from it.

She wouldn't have time to get out. Paralysed with fear, she leaned over the hole in the floor. Her eyes were streaming with stinging tears. Nicky was on the ground and the flames reflected in Jim's eyes as he looked up at her. If he waited to get her out, they would all die.

"Jim, save Nicky. I'll be ok. I'll just hop down myself," she lied.

In answer, Jim reached up and snagged her wrist. He could feel the rigidity in her tendons. She may not be able to jump down herself. There was no time to try and convince her, so he didn't bother trying. He just pulled her headfirst into the hole and deposited her on the soft dry dirt next to Nicholas.

"Problem solved," he said to her. "Now we can all leave."

The air was clearer, but it was still hard to breathe. There wasn't much time. The fire was rapidly spreading towards them, roaring like an angry beast and blocking the route out. Jim took Nicky and was glad that the little boy struggled at the enforced closeness. That meant he had not been as affected by the smoke as Jim had feared.

There was one more small problem. The area beneath the front bedrooms was completely sealed off from the street by decorative lattice work. Jim kicked at it until the diagonal strips of wood collapsed and they scrambled out into the garden. Ally was spent, but Jim half dragged her until they made it across the road and collapsed onto the cool grassy verge.

Ally would never forget the sound, the heat and the smell of her house as it continued to burn. A fire unit was already dousing the flames, turning it into a smouldering ruin.

For a few moments, they just sat, holding each other. Nicky played with the grass stems beside them. Ally looked at Jim with deep understanding. No matter what this man had done in the past, no matter who he really was or worked for, he had come back for them. He had saved them again and they were his for life. She had not made a mistake in trusting him. He was her hero.

"I love you," she breathed.

"I was just coming back to tell you that I love you too," he said as he kissed her gently on her blackened lips. He ruffled Nicky's hair. "And to tell you that you can't get rid of me that easily. I'm never leaving your side again."

"That's good, because I don't plan on ever letting you go."

The clapping of neighbours who had gathered to watch the fire reminded them that they were not alone.

"Charlie did it," she said with disbelief.

"His real name is Henry Charles," Jim told her. "I thought he looked familiar, but I didn't make the connection tight away. You don't expect to see the boss of one of the biggest crime organizations in Australia to be sitting on your front steps. The information on my background check of him just came through. Almost too late."

Ally couldn't believe what he was telling her. "Crime boss?"

"He is a nasty piece of work. Rumour has it that he never leaves his Melbourne compound, but I guess he does. Do you know why he did this?"

"It was something that happened a long time ago. Max was right. Charlie blamed him for the death of his son in an awful work accident. He thought that killing everyone Max loved would even the score. He is insane. Jim, where is he? He might come after us again."

"If he does, we'll be ready."

Ally shuddered, thinking of the vengeful old man and how nearly he ended their lives.

An ambulance arrived, sirens screaming. Seeing the soot smeared trio, both paramedics hurried over and ushered them to the ambulance. Ally waved them away from herself. Nicholas was more important. She stood close by, watching them work. Both men exuded a cheerful, almost jolly friendliness, casually tossing jokes around. Ally smiled. She didn't know how much was genuine and how much was designed to put their small patient and worried mother at ease, but it was working. They seemed so capable that she relaxed a bit.

They checked him carefully for skin burns and explained that they had to transport everyone to the nearest hospital to check them for inhalation burns.

"Oh no," Ally said, shaking her head. "I thought he was all right. You're telling me he may have internal burns?"

"Your son is probably fine, his oxygen level is great, but the doctors have to make sure. They'll probably have him under observation for about twenty-four hours."

Jim rode in the front of the ambulance with the driver, while Ally held Nicky's tiny hand in the back while he lay on a stretcher way too big for him with an oxygen mask on his face. He had been through so much already.

In the emergency department, all three were examined, so she and Nicky lay side by side in the same bed as nurses bustled about taking histories and checking their vital signs.

Jim was discharged, but Ally and Nicky spent the night in the children's ward. It was a cosy, warm, tiny world cut off from the rest of the universe where minutes merged into hours as everyone made the best of time away from home. Home. Ally found herself wondering where they would go when they were discharged. Their home was gone. She sighed as she realised that for the time being this was their home.

Nicky sat in his cot eating crumbed chicken pieces and she sat beside him, an unread magazine in her lap. A discrete knock on the door preceded two uniformed police officers. Ally was getting used to the routine. For twenty-seven years she had no contact at all with the law. Now she saw them almost every day and knew some of them by name. She even planned to spend her life with an ex-cop.

"Are you the owner of 242B Greyson Road?" he asked.

"Yes," Ally answered. "I was."

"Was there anyone else in the dwelling when it caught fire ma'am?" he asked, as if knowing the answer.

"Yes, my neighbour Charlie. Or rather Henry Charles. He started the fire. He wanted to kill us. But he escaped."

"No, we don't believe he did. The arson squad confirmed that they found human remains at the back of the house."

"And you think it was Charlie?"

"We can't be sure until the investigation is over, but we believe so."

Ally nodded quietly, feeling slightly sick while she imagined how Charlie suffered as he tried to escape the flames that he had lit. Sick but also relieved. It was finally over for him. His grief and hunger for vengeance were not something she could imagine living with. Long after the police had left and lights out signalled bedtime, Ally sat in the dark and relived the fire. When she finally fell asleep in the chair, she dreamt of fires starting all around her.

Jim came early the next day, before visiting hours and waited until the paediatrician had given Nicky a clean bill of health and discharged him. He had been busy, turning the fastback into a family car with the addition of a baby seat.

Ally asked him to take her to see the house one last time. The entire street looked different, even at a glance. The way a mouth looks with its front tooth missing.

The framework of her once beautiful house was the only thing left standing, while the yard had been cordoned off and danger signs posted. The sweet, sickly smell of burnt wood hung in the still, morning air.

Everything she owned was gone. All the mementoes, the photographs, all her beautiful things destroyed. Turned into wet, dirty ash. Tears streaked her cheeks. She hugged Nicholas tightly. The most important things in her life were safe. She just had to find a way to move forward.

Jim picked Nicky up and started walking to his car. Ally decided that it was time to clear the air between them. No more secrets.

"You must have seen this sort of thing many times in your work," she said, catching up to him.

Jim looked puzzled.

"When you were a policeman," she explained with a small smile.

"You knew?"

She nodded. "There is a lot I don't know though."

"Know that I will never lie to you again."

Ally smiled at him through a mist of tears, "I'm glad." She knew how hard it had been for him to keep the truth from her in the first place and she forgave him.

There was a long black car parked in front of Jim's car. Max Reed was standing beside his saloon. Despite the power of the man nicknamed the Lion, a loneliness and vulnerability lurked beneath the strong exterior. It made him more like Luke than she could have imagined. She finally understood the burden of pain that this man carried on his shoulders. The tragedy that enveloped him. She walked up to the big man and hugged him tightly, silently sending him a message of thanks and empathy. Then she stepped back and took Nicky from Jim.

"Come and meet your Uncle Max," she smiled at her brother-in-law as his face dissolved in tears. "You'll be seeing a lot of each other."

"Ally, Nicky. Let's go home." For once the deep voice sounded wobbly. "You'd better come too Conrad. It looks like you'll be part of this family too."

Ally linked an arm through each man's as they walked away from the charred ruin of what had been her home for so long. She felt only a vague relief at being left standing. After the shock wore off, maybe more emotions would surface. At the moment, relief was all she could handle. Looking up at Nicholas, riding high on his uncle's shoulders, a happy thought struck her.

"You," she said in a light voice, "are looking at an only child whose parents have always wanted two strong sons to complete their family. They are going to be so happy that I am finally going to indulge them. And such excellent specimens too. Can you take some time off from running your empire to meet my Mum and Dad? They're only 14 hours away."

Max considered her question for about 5 seconds, then grinning widely, he said, "what's the point of being the boss of a corporation if you can't take time off to visit the folks. And maybe less than 14 hours. I'll call my pilots to warm up the engines!"

EPILOGUE

Tiny waves lapped at the private jetty. A motor cruiser rocked gently on the water, its sleek white lines echoing the terraced house behind it. Ally shaded her eyes as she looked across the blue expanse to the distant Sydney Harbour Bridge. Even now, she was in awe of its size. And the beauty of the city she lived in.

The sound of laughter drew her attention to the glimmering pool below her. It was still too cold to swim, so Jim was helping Nicholas sail his new remote-controlled yacht over the turquoise water. She could hardly believe that her son would be starting school in the new year. He was becoming so tall and handsome, and when she looked at him, she would sometimes choke back tears of happiness. She had to work hard to stifle the urge to protect him from the world. The past was slowly dimming in her memory. The trauma of the kidnapping had mercifully let no mark on her little boy. But it had taken Ally a long time to recover. It took her months to even face a bath, let alone the sea. She saw strangers lurking in the shadows and had a recurring dream of flash fires breaking out all around her. Every time she would put one out, another would start, only closer and hotter. She would wake up gasping with sore lungs. Jim had been infinitely patient and loving. Nicholas loved him too.

The two were best of friends, Jim reliving the childhood he never had, they did everything together, especially now. Ally looked down at the tiny sleeping girl in her arms. A mass of curly blonde hair framed her tiny face as she breathed softly. Angelica was such a placid baby, but she could be demanding at times. She had only been with them a few short months, but she had changed all their lives.

Nicholas was full of the importance of being a big brother and was so gentle with her. Jim was still a little stunned. He treated his baby daughter as if she was made of the finest crystal and might break at any moment. Ally would catch him looking at his daughter as she slept with the strangest look on his face. Of wonder, matched with trepidation. Welcome to parenthood, she thought.

The baby stirred in her sleep and curled her fists. She frowned and then her face relaxed into blissful contentment.

Ally had chosen her name. An angel had helped her choose. She remembered the last time she had seen Luke and hoped he was happy wherever he was. A part of Luke lived on in her heart, in her memories and in his son. Often, she would imagine Nicholas as a grown man with a family of his own. Grandchildren with golden hair and blue eyes, playing at her feet and climbing onto her lap. She sighed blissfully at the thought.

"Mum! Mum! Look at this!" Nicholas waved to her as the yacht skimmed across the pool. Ally waved back to him, smiling. She exchanged looks with Jim. Never would she have believed that it was possible to love someone so much.

Jim's current investigation was based here in Sydney. The director of the company he was scrutinising had given them the use of this incredible house. It was easy to grow accustomed to this luxury. But soon they would have to move on. After the fire, Ally had not wanted to start again. She had been content to follow Jim wherever he travelled, living like gypsies with only three suitcases to their name. They had spent over six months on her parents' farm. Her mother instantly claimed Jim as the son she never had and made apple pie and hazelnut cookies to fatten him up. Her father put away his books to play with his grandson and to take him for long walks around the farm. Their once immaculate house was strewn with toys and her mother refused any offers to tidy up. She said there would be time enough for that later.

Together they would sit on the porch swing, watching the men outside and give thanks for the way things had turned out. Even Max had flown out for Christmas. He seemed more at peace with himself but his loneliness was heartbreaking. One of the reasons they had returned to Australia was to spend more time with Max.

Now that Nicholas was ready to start school, it was time to settle down. And Ally was ready. Her fingers itched to paint, to plan, to decorate. This time she would have open spaces and huge windows. Windows that would never be barred. It would be a home that reflected the love within. Carefully packed in a large crate, the first of her purchases awaited. It was a very large, very ornate, grandfather clock. She wasn't sure she could handle the bells every hour, but was looking forward to trying.

Ally gently placed Angelica into her bassinette. She picked up her wide brimmed straw hat and made her way carefully down the terraces to the pool.

"You boys look like you are having fun," she said as she approached them.

Nicholas ran up and hugged her tightly around her waist. "Oh yes Mum, we sure are. This boat is so neat. How long will it be until Angelica can play?"

Ally laughed, "A few years yet, sweetheart."

"Babies aren't much fun. They never do anything exciting." With that he ran off the far end of the pool where the yacht floated, becalmed.

Jim put his arm around her shoulders and they stood watching the little boy. "One day, we'll have to tell him."

"I know, but not yet. He's too young."

"You underestimate him, Ally. He's a brave young man, just like his mother. Besides…"

"Besides what?"

"It would be like an adventure story to him. He'd love to hear how exciting his time as a baby was."

"I guess so."

"Have I told you how much I love you? You and Nicky and Angelica are my reason for living. My family."

Ally kissed him lightly. "And you are mine, ours. I love you, Jim Conrad." As she closed her eyes and leant her head on his shoulder, an unimaginable peace and happiness flowed through her. She was home.

THE END